BOOK #1 IN TH... S

THE CAT THAT CHASED CADILLACS

BOOK#1 IN THE BLACK CAT DETECTIVE AGENCY SERIES

THE CAT THAT CHASED CADILLACS

G. DAVID STIRLING

BLACK CAT DETECTIVE AGENCY PRESS © 2024 by G. David Stirling

Copyright © 2024 by G. David Stirling

All rights reserved.

No part of this publication may be reproduced, distributed, or transmitted in any form or by any means, including photocopying, recording, or other electronic or mechanical methods, without the prior written permission of the publisher, except as permitted by U.S. copyright law. For permission requests, contact the author at davidstirlingauthor@gmail.com.

ISBN: 9798337857237

The story, all names, characters, and incidents portrayed in this production are fictitious. No identification with actual persons (living or deceased), places, buildings, and products is intended or should be inferred.

First edition 2024

10 9 8 7 6 5 4 3 2

ACKNOWLEDGEMENT

In no way could this book have ever been completed without the constant advice, support, suggestions, encouragement, and sleep deprivation from my wonderful wife, Teri.

DEDICATION

This book is dedicated to two feline creatures that rescued me a decade ago. Locke, who was with me at my keyboard every day, until one day, he wasn't. And Panther, his brother, who is the inspiration for the character you are about to meet — B. Buckleberry.

Mt. Medallion
State Park

Red Barn Christmas Tree Farm

Police Station

Shaw's House

Dale Sharpe Cadillac

Route 16

TOWN OF
Copper Summit

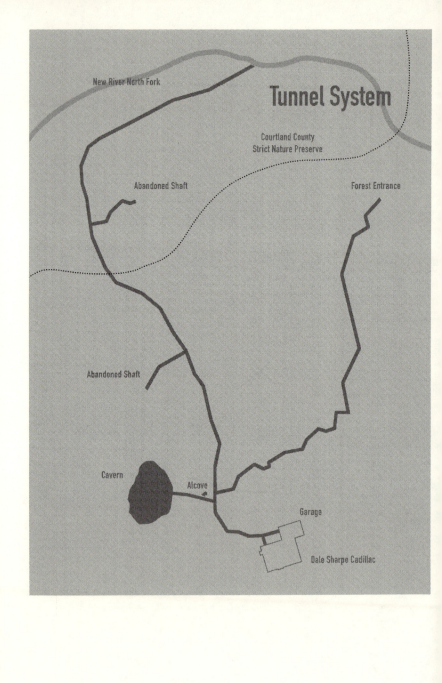

TABLE OF CONTENTS

The Office Under The Shed	1
Plankk Case Solved	7
Luzhkov	15
Mr. Tuttle	21
King Of Cadillacs	27
Townsend Media	31
Studio	37
Action	43
CSPD Coffee Break	47
Catnip & Crooks	51
Going For A Ride	59
Road Trip	63
Dark Forest	67
Tunnel	71
Snowstorm	75
Dealership	81
Dumpster	89
Mrs. Baer	93
INTERPOL Report	99
Courtland County Map	105
Catnap	111

Mr. Baer	117
Collision	123
Valerie	127
Office Hours	133
Answers	141
Back to the Office	147
Into the Shed	151
Power	155
Lev	163
Lev Talks	169
Firefight	173
Service Bay	179
Oil Painting	183
Into The Fire	191
Showroom Floor	195
Tunnels	201
Branches	207
Alcove	213
Den of Thieves	217
Improvisation	223
Death Wish	229
A Long Walk	235
Ruins	241
CSPD	251
Doormat	257

PART ONE
COPPER SUMMIT

CHAPTER 1

The Office Under The Shed

I was sitting at my desk, finishing the last bits of Lickers® gelled tuna from a long pink tube. Not the best snack, but I hadn't eaten since my humans put down my morning bowl, so it would have to do.

I'd pulled the file on the Plankk case from my desk drawer. Going over the facts I'd written down and looking at the sketches I'd made, I finally realized what I needed. I headed to my tiny kitchen and put on some water to boil.

It is a well-known fact that cats — not dogs, not horses, not even those big furry birds that can talk — yes, cats are the most intelligent species that God has ever put on this Earth. Even if one were to consider a human being, that most complex collection of cells and synapses, what comes to mind? Greed, deception, and a general lack of compassion for their fellow man. Yes, of course, there is the occasional kindness, but more often than not, humans will find themselves in 'self-preservation' mode, which belies all of their other intentions, good or bad.

I have an innate knowledge of these things, for I am that aforementioned creature, the cat. And a black one at that. I've spent my whole life weaving between these humans' legs, purring in their laps, joining them as they use the facilities, covertly watching for predators. Perhaps they've been unaware of my sentience, probably so. They've undoubtedly had no inkling of my comings and goings while away at work or on vacation. I can certainly take care of myself for at least a week at a time when they're away, yet they insist on hiring someone to 'look in' on me. I guess it makes them feel better. Or less guilty. The fact is, human vacations are when I do my best work. Crime-solving is a delicate career indeed, and it's most fruitful without the constant interruptions of chin scratchings and belly rubs.

When William Shaw decided to build a larger utility shed in our backyard, I contracted out for some work of my own to be done. Lenny from Woodchuck Construction gave me a great deal — one custom office with a small kitchen in exchange for my detective services at any point in the future. It was only a day's work for him and his crew, so he considered it fair. Once the shed was up and the Shaws were gone for a weekend, Lenny and his crew hollowed out the underneath, constructed my new office, and then paneled everything in a very aromatic knotty pine.

Business was good, but having my own office made things easier for me — no more birds, chipmunks, or even dogs coming into the house through my cat door to meet in the sunroom while the Shaws were out. As if my job wasn't hard enough, a couple of sets of muddy paw prints from the Bernese down the street had taken me practically an hour to clean. So, the office afforded me space to work away from the main house should any prying eyes happen to notice my midnight excursions. My office door faced away from the house, hidden behind a set of thick bushes. On the front, the raven,

Ellery, who had done all the intricate woodwork around the office had chiseled into the green pine the words: B. BUCKLEBERRY. And beneath that, BLACK CAT DETECTIVE AGENCY.

The office itself was rather small, but it suited me. Maybe the shelves of books surrounding the office on every wall made it seem tight. But needless to say, books were a necessity. The fireplace and hearth were on the long outside wall, right by my desk, perfect for the colder weather. I didn't know of any other cats who had such a nice space to work. Finally, the kettle whistled.

When I needed to think, I'd sip an Earl Grey, nipped, of course. I had a robust selection of cat nips perched along the top of the stove in small porcelain jars, along with a cabinet full of international teas and a small selection of coffees. I picked a Persian catmint nip that always invigorated me when pondering a case. Putting the tea bag in my mug and sprinkling it with the nip, I poured the water over the top and carefully brought it to my desk, a wooden stirring spoon resting inside.

The R. Plankk matter was my first unsolved case. I refunded the client, a Mister Rathbone Plankk, the initial charge. I felt that it was unfair for a vole to hand over my requested fee just for me to tell him that I had no idea who stole his priceless 1952 Picasso sketch of a woman with two milk jugs, which had been hanging in his underground study.

"Did Picasso ever paint this piece?" I asked the first time I met him. Cats don't typically eat voles, and while I was tempted to bat him around a bit, I had to maintain a professional demeanor.

"He did," said Mr. Plankk. His voice was very high and somewhat pathetic and sad.

"What was it called?" I took a thick art book down from my library, put it on the desk, and started to leaf through it with my paws.

"Woman With Two Milk Jugs."

"Of course."

After a minute of searching, I found it. "Ah yes, here it is. Seems the original painting is hanging in a museum in Milan. Where did you get the sketch, Mr. Plankk?"

"I found it near the curb of the art gallery in Sturbridge, someone must have dropped it. I took it back to my hole, and it had been hanging in my study for years until last night. I'm heartbroken. Voles don't often get anything of value, living underground and such. I mean, things get dirty. But I pinned it to the wall and straightened it every afternoon."

So that's how the meeting with my client went. That very day, I walked around town, talking to some of the critters around the vole's underground domicile, sniffing around both entrances, trying to detect a scent different from Mr. Rathbone Plankk or his family. I could not. I also interviewed and smelled the wife, Tilde. I, of course, could not fit into the vole tunnel to examine the crime scene, so I had little to go on. I followed up on a few leads over the following days, but eventually, I had to call Mr. Plankk into my office to give him the bad news. By refunding his fee of one new shiny dime, a felt toy mouse, and a crunchy leaf, I had hoped he would not tell the neighborhood how poorly the investigation had gone. He understood and went back to his Picasso-less den. And it's been bothering me ever since.

But last night, I fell asleep to the wind blowing leaves past my window. I dreamt of running through the woods, chasing them, leaping high into the air and trying to catch one. And when I woke, that's when it hit me.

So, I looked over the Plankk case once more. Everything lined up. The next step was to get in contact with the vole himself. I opened the front door and called out.

"Ariella!" I stepped away from the door, leaving it open, and went back to sit at my desk, sipping from my tea, which was now unpleasantly lukewarm.

After a moment or two, a beak peeked in.

"Ariella, it's fine. Please come in." Her head twitched to the right, her black eyes looking around my office. "Please. I promise you're safe." She put one foot forward, and then I could see her yellow body. I put my mug down on the desk with a thud, and immediately, she stepped back outside, scared.

"Wait, look." I reached behind me into a small silver bucket and picked up a long, juicy worm in my paw. She stepped into the office and gingerly walked to the front of my desk, ducking her head with every step. I threw the worm to her, and she caught it in her beak, gulping it down within a second.

"Can you please retrieve Mr. Plankk, the vole, for me…" I started, but then, involuntarily, my words changed to chitters, little chirps almost, that I could not control. I cleared my throat and tried again.

"Ahh, the umm, the vole, Mr. Plankk, I need you to…" And now my tail. It twitched back and forth, snapping this way and that. The golden bird slowly moved toward the open door, never taking her eyes off me. I had a small envelope that I tossed to her, and it landed by her feet.

"I'm sorry, Ariella. It's just that, I c-c-c-c-c-c-c-c-can't really c-c-c-c-c-control it, but I promise I won't hurt you…" My tail snapped again, and I held it down with my paw. "Just get Mr. Plankk to c-c-c-c-c-c-come by, please, and I'll give you another worm."

Ariella was truly the most reliable messenger in all of Copper Summit. I had tried pigeons, parrots, and US Postal, but she was, by far, the fastest and cheapest. USPS wanted 73 cents for a stamp. That was more than my daily rate.

She picked up the envelope in her beak, bowed her head, and with a quick hop was out the door.

CHAPTER 2

Plankk Case Solved

There was a timid knock at the door. "Please, Mr. Plankk, come in."

The door squeaked open, and Rathbone Plankk squeaked through the small gap, squeaking a frightened, "Hello."

I extended my paw, indicating that there was a small leather chair in front of my desk that might offer him comfort while we spoke. He slowly climbed up into it and put his small hands in his lap. Clearing my throat, I asked if he might like some tea. I didn't mention the catnip. That was mine.

"Oh, no, no, I had tea earlier this morning. But thank you," he replied.

A tapping at the door. Oh, Ariella, I had forgotten. "Coming, coming," I told her.

A quick opening of the door, the quick tossing of a worm into the dirt outside, and I didn't have to be tempted by a delicious juicy bird coming into my office, and Ariella didn't have to be worried about a possible pouncing cat. Not that I would ever do such a thing. So, the decision to keep things at arm's reach made everyone happy. I sat back down at my desk.

"Very well. Thank you for coming down. I would have made the trip to you, but it's very difficult for a creature of my size to— well, it's impossible for me — to actually fit into your house. Though I'm sure it's very nice."

"Oh, yes. Mrs. Plankk has certainly made our house into a home."

"Let's talk about your home for a moment. You have an entrance as well as an exit, is that correct?" I put my paw on my chin as I always did while verbalizing my theories. In this case, though, I was almost sure this was no longer a theory.

"Yes, Mr. Buckleberry. They're both hidden though, you know, predators and all."

"I would imagine that sometimes, when atmospheric conditions are just right, you can get a very pleasant breeze that travels through the house. Is that correct?"

"Oh, yes. In the summertime, it is quite enjoyable."

"And in the winter?"

"Well, we close it up at both ends in the winter and only go out as needed. For groceries and such."

I put on my reading glasses and looked through my paperwork, flipping pages back and forth. "You say that the robbery occurred in the month of July, the 25th, is that correct?" I looked down at him over the edge of my glasses.

"That would be, yes, that would be right. Sometime in the afternoon. Both Tilde and I were out, and Jeremy had just come home from school, frantic. He let himself in."

"Oh, there are doors on your tunnel?"

"Well, um, no. I mean, he went inside."

"Is there anything you remember about that day, Mr. Plankk? Besides the robbery, of course?"

The vole sat in the chair, scratching his head with a sharp, curved claw. "Well, yes, I suppose we had a strong storm move through the area. We had some wind damage to the roof at the insurance shop, I remember."

"Where you work?"

"Yes."

I collected the papers in front of me, gathering them together and tamping them down onto the surface of the desk. "I believe that I've solved your case, Mr. Plankk." I put the papers into the manila folder marked PLANKK — STOLEN PICASSO.

"Have you now?"

"Yes. Allow me to recount the events as I believe they unfolded."

"Oh, please do," said Mr. Plankk, moving a bit toward the edge of the oversized (for him) chair.

"That afternoon, as you say, a powerful storm came through Courtland County, bringing with it rain and heavy winds. Now, your home, well-built as it is, suffered no damage from the rain because of how the ingress and egress are constructed on raised hillocks, with each opening under a small plant, covering it from the rain. However, your home, like your place of work, was not immune to the effects of the wind that day."

"You don't say…" The little vole hunched forward even more.

"All it would take would be one heavy gust to blow through your house, to lift that paper sketch from its pin in the wall, and send it fluttering to the floor. And there it sat, with the pin laying in the corner of the room, until your son Jeremy came home, frantic. And why was he frantic, Mr. Plankk?"

"Well, he was going to a birthday party for one of his friends after school, and he forgot to wrap his present..."

"Which was?" I asked.

"A set of finger paints for his friend Knox."

"A fox?"

"Umm, no, sir, a chicken."

"I see. So, Jeremy comes home, gets his box of finger paints from his room, looks for wrapping paper, knowing he's missing the party, searching everywhere, when all of a sudden, why, there's some right there on the floor!"

"My Picasso!"

"Correct. Jeremy, carefully and lovingly, I'm sure, wraps his friend's gift in your priceless sketch, not knowing, of course, and runs out of your home to the birthday party where the gifts are opened, the cake is eaten, and games are played. And afterward, all of the trash, including all of the wrapping paper from Knox's presents, is disposed of."

"Oh. Dear."

"But our story is not over. Might I ask, of what occupation is Knox's father?"

Plankk thought for a bit. "Hmm. I believe he repairs televisions and the like."

"And his mother?" I pulled a large volume off one of the shelves, mint green and quite heavy. This was one from the turn of the last century: *A Pictorial Encyclopedia Of The Animal Kingdom.* Licking my paw, I flipped to the chicken section.

"Oh, she's a stay-at-home chicken," replied Plankk.

"I believe I've seen her before. She's a Japanese Bantam, no?" I showed Plankk the picture in the encyclopedia—a thin, long-feathered black and white bird with very short legs. The vole leaned up to take a look.

"Ah yes, that's her, that's the one. Quite fetching."

"I wonder if she has any hobbies. Drawing? Painting? Perhaps, origami?"

Plankk thought. "Why yes, funny you should mention. After the birthday party, Jeremy brought home a gift she had made, an origami flying chicken. It's hanging in his room. It was the only thing that brought a smile to my face that night... why..." As Plankk began to put the pieces together, he lifted his tiny eyes to mine. "You don't mean to say..."

"Perhaps you should check and see if your son's flying chicken is, in fact, your priceless Picasso."

Mr. Plankk leapt up from the chair and again up to the desk, shaking my hand repeatedly.

"Why yes! Of course! Thank you, Mr. Buckleberry. Thank you!"

It was almost 6, and my family would be home. They start to call for me when it gets dark as if I cannot take care of myself, so I like to be close by to avoid the embarrassment of having the neighborhood hear them calling for 'Mr. Buckles'. It's shameful.

My family, the Shaws, live in a very nice and very old Victorian. It is one of the only houses of its kind here in Courtland County. Because of the remote location of our little town, Copper Summit, it was very costly to transport wood and supplies up into the mountains a hundred years back. So, most houses were just squares that were framed out and added to over the years. Once the railroad came and more and more roads gave access to most of the county, newer homes were built, but the Victorian style at that point was a thing of the past.

Funny how it worked out, but the original builder of the house was a judge for Courtland County, Judge H. Lee Harris. Over the decades, it was passed down to his descendants until Detective William H. Shaw bought it. Apparently, he is a well-respected, well-liked member of the community. He's thought of highly, from what I read in the papers that sometimes line my box. It makes me wonder if they pick out those articles specifically. Detective Shaw reminds me of one of those rugged old Hollywood actors I see on the movie posters at the Parkway Theater downtown.

He wasn't home yet, but Mrs. Shaw and the children were.

Catherine Shaw is a very nice woman who always keeps my bowl in the kitchen full. I think humans would consider her pretty. She has red hair that she keeps short, in a flop, blip, or bob, or whatever they call it. She's a little shorter than her husband, and she's a teacher at the elementary school. I know this because every August, she scrambles to get her classroom ready and shoos me off the dining room table where I like to lie in the sun. The placemats make perfect beds, so much better than the 'real' ones they continually buy for me. But she throws her supplies everywhere until there's no longer room for the furriest member of the family, and then I end up on the floor, looking for another spot. Like I said, humans lack compassion at times.

Then there's Francesca, Frannie, who hates her name. I hear her complain about it all the time. She has red hair like her mother, but much longer, and she likes to yell and scream and be mean to her little brother, Patrick. I hear her parents say that they're never going to have another child again.

Patrick, the youngest, is my favorite. He doesn't yell like his sister, and he likes to gently pet me. In the right direction, from the head down. He never jumps up and startles me, never screams to wake me from a pleasant dream, and never ignores me if I rub up against his leg. And he doesn't move around much when he's sleeping, so he's very warm to curl up against. He gives me more treats than anyone else, too. I'm pretty certain he likes me.

As Mrs. Shaw set my bowl down, Frannie began to tell everyone about her absolutely horrible day. I ate.

The front door opened with a blast of cold air. I looked up from my bowl and turned my head. Detective Shaw appeared, closing the door behind him, his scarf flapping in the draft.

"We need to go. Now."

CHAPTER 3

Luzhkov

The Highlander Motel accepted pets. I was very glad of that. The two-mile trip in my crate had upset my stomach, but for the time being, I kept my dinner where it belonged. Travel was so much easier when I was outside the crate — I didn't get car sick and I could see so much more. Catherine was afraid I'd run away, and if we were going to the vet, she'd probably be right. But if that were to ever happen, I'd always come home. The vet wasn't far. So the ride here was anything but reassuring, and I was thankful for the grey catnip mouse that Patrick had thrown into my crate.

"I'm sorry, honey," said Shaw to his wife. "There's just no way around it. We'll stay at the motel tonight, maybe tomorrow, and then, as long as it's safe, we'll go back home. But I have no idea what he'll do, and I'm not taking any chances."

He had explained to Mrs. Shaw earlier, as they were packing, about their current predicament. I listened from the kitchen, then as they moved to the living room, and then up into the bedroom where suitcases were opened and clothes thrown into them.

"He's unpredictable, Catherine, a loose cannon. We know he's killed before. And I'm the one who sent him down to State the first time. Now that he's been released, who knows what's going to happen."

"What about the State Police outside the house?"

"Listen, I know this guy. I've gone over his history, his record, his life. Hun, he is not a good guy."

"Okay…"

"Please trust me. After a few days, once we get a bead on him and know his whereabouts and patterns, then we can make an informed decision. But for now, I think this is our best option. I'm truly sorry. Someone can cover for you at school?"

"…at least until the end of the week…" Mrs. Shaw replied, her voice shaking.

As they packed the car, the children asked a million questions their father refused to answer. Francesca was, of course, upset that she'd be away from her friends for a few days. Patrick wanted to know if he could carry one of his father's weapons, you know, just in case. He looked at this as some kind of great adventure, which made his father set his jaw and not say much more about things.

Detective Shaw made sure everyone was settled, and then the Suburban pulled away from the house. The snow came down into the headlights like we were flying through stars. Patrick reached into the top of my crate through one of the slots and scratched my head. I nuzzled back against him. I think all of us were scared, though none of us really knew what was going on.

It was only in the dark hours of the morning, as Patrick and Frannie lay sleeping in one of the motel's queen beds, and Mr. and Mrs. Shaw talked in the other, that I came to understand what was happening.

There was a man. His name was Lev Luzhkov. The things that Mr. Shaw told his wife were, well, disturbing. I'm sure he only scratched the surface, not wanting to scare her too much but wanting to impart just how dangerous this man was and how careful she should be over the next few days. Lev sounded like someone that you would cross the street to avoid. Maybe that's an understatement. Lev sounded like someone you'd uproot your family for and hide yourself away for a few days just to make sure your paths did not cross.

Obviously, he was Russian mob, or at least Eastern European. Six months after he was released from NC State Prison, which the actions and testimony of Detective Shaw had put him in years prior, he was arrested again for attempted murder. The supposed hit was on a small-time Russian bookie up in Kelso 30 miles up the road. The arresting officer, however, had read the Miranda rights in English, which according to Mr. Luzhkov's lawyer, Mr. Luzhkov did not understand. Imprisoned for 32 days, he had to be released on that technicality. And now, Detective Shaw figured he and his family were target number one on Luzhkov's hit list.

"I've got my records, everything that this guy's been charged with, even in Russia," he said. "Catherine, let's just take this time to relax and figure out our next move."

"Relax?" hissed Mrs. Shaw, trying to keep her voice down in the dark hotel room. "Seriously, Will? Relax?"

"I know, I know, it's... it's crazy. But we've got protection. We've got a Statie outside our room and one at the house, so we're covered. I don't want you to worry about that."

"Well, I'm worried. Sorry, but I am. This is... it's just, it's not right."

"I know..." Shaw held his wife as I watched them, my head resting on my paws, pretending I was asleep like the kids. My eyes, halfway shut, darted to the door. Mr. Shaw had put a steel safety bar between the knob and the floor. I looked at the plate glass window, shades drawn. An elbow could smash it in.

"Look, I'm probably just overthinking this. But I wanted to be sure. Okay?"

They hugged each other a little tighter.

"I don't like it," Catherine said.

"I don't either."

They brought my box with them and kept it under the sink just outside the bathroom. The Highlander Motel was nothing special, just a room with two queen beds, a small refrigerator, and a large double window that looked out over a small parking area and Mt. Medallion miles away in the distance.

Detective Shaw left close to sunrise. I was not allowed outside, though I did howl at the door the first few hours after dawn. First, Mrs. Shaw shooed me away, and then Frannie told me to stop being a baby and got a slipper thrown at me, but then Patrick picked me up and played with me on the bed, swinging a small feathered bird on a piece of elastic tied to a stick. Of course I knew it wasn't real, but it was fun to bat at it when it swung past me and kept my reflexes sharp. Every once in a while I'd grab it and keep it, letting my back paws dig into the thing while I made sure it was dead with my teeth.

"Mom, please, can we go somewhere? This is boring!" complained Frannie. She sat down on the bed in a huff and made me bounce up a bit. I jumped down off the bed.

"When your father says it's safe. I told you to bring books. And you have your phone." She peered out from the curtains. I sprung up into the window with her. The black and white was parked a few doors down, facing out. Two officers sat inside, one of them drinking coffee from the motel's lobby. I liked coffee. Hopefully, Mrs. Shaw would make some soon from the room's coffee pot, and I could sneak a lick or two before she lifted me away.

The snow from last night was already starting to melt. Not much had stuck to the road, but it made the forest that surrounded us sparkle and shine. The ledge was cold, but I settled onto it to look outside as the early morning sun made everything glow white.

Coming from the left, from the wooded entrance to the motel, was a car, sleek and long and old, the kind that you just don't see on the road anymore. Tail fins. Curved windshield that would probably cost a small fortune to replace. And it was cream, almost matching the snow. It glided into the small drive like a shark, passing the patrol car. I hoped at least one of the officers in the car had taken notice and was checking on the plate number. It approached our room and the only thing I could see through the tinted passenger window was an orange dot, glowing. A cigarette or cigar, I figured. The darkness of the glass prevented me from seeing anything else.

I looked at the patrolmen in the parked police vehicle, but it seemed business as usual for them. Talking, laughing. Sipping coffee. The old car made a wide loop at the end of the parking lot, leaving tire tracks in the snow. In North Carolina, you only need a plate at the rear of your vehicle, but snow and ice from the night's squall left the license plate almost unreadable. But I did manage to see one small word at the top of the plate above the tag number:

DEALER

The car finished its turn and left as silently as it came.

CHAPTER 4

Mr. Tuttle

It was easy enough for me to slip out the motel room door unnoticed when Catherine shouted out to the cops in the car, asking if they needed anything. I'm sure at some point one of the kids, probably Patrick, would notice I was no longer there and mention it to his mom. But they know I'm more than capable of handling myself outside, even in the cold.

However, the first thing I noticed when I slipped between Mrs. Shaw's legs was the temperature of the snow. I almost meowed, but I kept quiet and ran into the trees. The first thing I needed to do was get onto the pavement where the sun at least would have warmed up the road. It would be a little wet, but I had towels at the office.

Last night, once everyone fell asleep, I jumped onto the nightstand and knocked Shaw's files to the floor. The papers scattered. I jumped down and started reading. Within a minute, I was sure that Shaw had done the right thing.

Among the papers was a face staring back at me — chiseled, cruel, as ugly as a boxer's from the 1920s. It was grainy and small, but there was no mistaking that this was a dangerous man. I read on.

Lev Luzhkov was a career criminal, a checkered past back in Russia, and some prison time here in the states. His history was captured in the first few paragraphs. After being suspected of murder at 17 years of age in his hometown of Sokol, a port town in Siberia, he escaped in the fish hold of a trawler bound for Japan. He then somehow overpowered the three crewmen on board and piloted the craft to the shores of Alaska by himself. He ran the trawler aground near Nome, and from there, he begged, borrowed, and stole his way to North Carolina, 4000 miles away. Why? There was nothing here in these pages that gave me the answer to that. He was suspected in a number of murders in some of the major cities in the state, most likely drug-related. Then, about four years ago, he was captured on a weapons charge when he fired into the ceiling of a nightclub in Raleigh-Durham, allegedly trying to intimidate members of some overseas criminal organization, who unfortunately escaped. Chaos ensued, patrons were trampled, all of it caught on video.

Even though I was just a kitten when this occurred, I remembered it. Shaw had been in Raleigh for two weeks of intensive training before his promotion to Detective, and he was one of several officers to answer the 911 call at the nightclub. He was also the officer who took Luzhkov down, almost breaking his arm in the ensuing scuffle before he was cuffed and arrested. Shaw sat directly behind Luzhkov during the preliminary hearing. Luzhkov was in prison until his trial date.

Discharging a firearm within an enclosure with the intent to incite fear is a Class F felony. The prosecution had reached a deal that threw out other charges if the State could make this one stick. And it did. The judge gave Luzhkov the maximum penalty of 33 months in jail. After hearing the sentence, Luzhkov had to be tased as he leapt behind him to attack Detective Shaw. Another six months was added to his jail time without the possibility of parole. None of this had been mentioned to Mrs. Shaw.

As I jogged along the warmer road, my thick coat keeping me warm, I wondered why this man had come all the way across the country, stealing and probably killing as he went. What did this part of America hold for him? Or was it just coincidence... keep running until he found a place to settle? None of it made any sense to me. Could that have been him in the old car I saw from the window last night? Smoking a fat cigar and wondering how and when to take out my owner, Detective Shaw? Something had to be done.

My plan was this: first, get back to my office and look up that car. Figure out the make and model of it. And then, second, visit my friend at the station and see what she could dig up. I was looking forward to that part.

A half hour later and I was turning off the main road and into the Shaw's small neighborhood. At this point, I no longer followed the road but ran in a straight line over hills, jumping gates and crawling under bushes until I came to our wooded backyard. And the door to my office at the back end of the shed. I was wet and cold and tired.

There was someone waiting for me in front of the small green door — a turtle. I didn't know any turtles. I slowed my pace and walked up to him, ducking under the bush that hid the little door.

"Hello, may I help you?" I asked, hoping this would be a quick matter so I could research the car as soon as possible.

"I do hope you can," the turtle said slowly. "Miss Wellington sent me." His voice was little more than a soft croak.

"Ah. The porcupine."

"Yes. Well, her sister."

"Miss Wellington's sister sent you?"

"Yes. Miss Wellington." This was all getting rather confusing.

"I see. Well, it's cold and damp out here, how about we talk inside?" I opened the door, holding it open for my guest, who took forever to get his body through as I stood there shivering. I counted to about fifty and then finally had the room to step around the turtle. When I entered the office, I darted into the kitchen to grab a towel. I came back into the study, toweling myself off, rubbing my legs as I stuck them out at odd angles to make sure I was dry everywhere.

"Now, what seems to be the problem, Mister…"

"Mister Tuttle."

"Yes, Mister Tuttle. Miss Wellington recommended my services?"

"She did. Though she heard of you through her sister, Miss Wellington."

I continued drying myself, not wanting to go down that road again. "So tell me, how can I help?" I put the towel over my shoulder, and set some kindling into the small fireplace. Upon lighting it, I threw some birch bark on top and sat in my leather chair, drying my face with the towel.

"I live on the riverbank, Mr. Buckleberry. I've made a very nice home there over the past, oh, 20 years or so. I take sticks and leaves and brush, and I've built a little piece of heaven there on the sides of the New River, sir. You should see it. It's very…"

"Yes, yes, I understand. Does this concern your house?" I finished drying my head with the towel and dropped it to the floor.

"I should say so!" said Mr. Tuttle, raising his head in indignation. "Like I said, it's quite a lovely property and…"

"And has something happened to it?"

"It most certainly has!"

"What's happened to your house, Mr. Tuttle?"

"Why, it's no longer there! It's gone!"

"Are you saying someone stole your house?" At this point, I was even more confused than I was about the Wellington sisters.

"Yes, that is what I'm saying. If one's house is there one day and not the next, how can there be any other explanation?" He tried to cross his arms to make a point but found he couldn't.

"Well," I started, "there could be any number of explanations for such a thing, Mr. Tuttle, a flood, for example, or say, umm, maybe a human came along and trampled it by mistake…"

"That's all well and good, but I build my houses fine and strong!"

"I'm sure you do, I wasn't saying…"

"Oh, what a waste of time. Someone steals your house, and no one cares. Lifts it right up and steals it. What's a turtle to do? Talk to a cat? How ridiculous."

"Well, I'm sorry you feel that way, sir…"

"Bah! What do cats know about turtles?"

"Mr. Tuttle, I solve crimes. I don't necessarily need to know the specifics concerning each species…"

"You are no help whatsoever! Absolutely none!"

I wasn't quite sure what to say. "Then... I'm sorry I couldn't help you. Please give Miss Wellington, the ah, the other Miss Wellington, my regards."

"I shall not! Good day, sir!" Mr. Tuttle said, and slowly stepping down from the height of the chair, he made his way onto the wooden floor and then slowly moved to the door over a period of about a minute or two. One short appendage after the other. I left my desk, squeezed by him, and opened the door for him, standing next to it. He made little clicks on the floor as he walked and turned his head slowly to look at me one last time as if a final dismissal were in order. I watched him putter forward, eventually making it to the threshold of the door, where he continued walking until his body finally was outside. I nodded goodbye and closed and locked the door.

I exhaled and looked at my vast library. Following my paw, I looked down the middle row, and there it was — my volume on cars: *Barrett's Encyclopedia of American Cars of the 20th Century.*

The vehicle that came through the motel parking lot was surely from the '50s, possibly early '60s. I flipped to that section, licking my paw when the pages stuck together. Studebakers, Corvairs, DeSotos.... Wait, there it was. I turned back a page. Though this one was black, it was definitely the car I saw. A 1958 Cadillac Coupe DeVille. Tail fins and a double set of headlights at the front. Who might have such a classic car as this one in a remote town like Copper Summit? There was only one answer.

Dale Sharpe, King of Cadillacs.

CHAPTER 5

King Of Cadillacs

"It's me, Dale Sharpe, King of Cadillacs, and, boy, do I have an offer for you! This 2020 Cadillac CT5, low mileage — a honey of a deal at only twenty-seven eight ninety-five! That's right, twenty-seven eight ninety-five only at Dale Sharpe in Copper Summit!"

My head tilted up. I was just finishing up some expense reports with the TV on in the background. Mr. Sharpe's delivery was quick, showy, and almost haphazardly edited together, as if he could not get all the words out in one take, so several had to be combined. It was a sloppy job, yet these commercials seemed to work for him. Everyone knew the King of Cadillacs around these parts, and when people saw him in restaurants or walking the streets downtown, they would stop and shake hands, sometimes taking pictures with their spouses or children. He was a friendly man, thin, tall, and wiry, and just like in his commercials, he always seemed as if he had one too many cups of coffee that morning. I'd often seen him in town, greeting the townsfolk with a smile or a chuckle at a joke he made.

When it was warm, and my travels would take me down to Main Street, I'd hear Dale say, "Hot enough for ya?" many times over. In the winter, I could be sure that The King of Cadillacs would shake hands with everyone who came up to him and say, "Cold enough for ya?" Then, he'd laugh and pretend to listen to what the other person had to say while figuring out a way to extract himself from the conversation. That's what I thought anyway, though it's true that I'm skeptical of any type of human behavior. Except for Patrick, of course. And maybe Shaw.

Where would a 1958 Cadillac Coupe DeVille come from if not Dale Sharpe, King of Cadillacs? It's not like there were a ton of car dealerships here of any make. The closest car lot besides Dale's was down the mountain, 32 miles away. And another thing I'd just remembered, Dale loved to collect cars. He supposedly had a hangar full of them. Though I've never seen it, it was rumored to be like a museum. Is this where the DeVille came from?

I couldn't really use a phone, not with my paws. I had some luck with a rotary in the past, but there was no way I'd be able to get Atlantic Wireless to install a landline here at the back of the shed. The only luck I'd had was on flip phones with sturdy keys. They're just hard to come by now. For some reason, smartphones did not recognize the pads of my paws. Horrible design flaw. I did, however, have a fairly new Dell with an oversized keyboard that I could type with. Which meant that I could 'chat' with Sharpe Cadillac's customer service center. I looked at the time. 4:40 pm. They still had a few minutes left on the clock.

Typing in their URL, I started a chat with Jennifer C. I was next in the queue. The keys clicked as I typed in my first and last name. Beckett Buckleberry.

JENNIFER C: Hello, Mr. Buckleberry, how may I help you?

BUCKLEBERRY: Hello! I am having an issue with my car and Mr. Sharpe had said if I had any problems to dial his personal cell phone but I seem to have misplaced his card and I don't see his number on the website

JC: (After a moment's hesitation) Yes, Mr. Sharpe does give that out occasionally, but unfortunately, I'm not allowed to pass that information on to others, Mr. Buckleberry

BB: Oh. Well. That is unfortunate

JC: He'll be in the office tomorrow if you'd like to come by.

BB: I might just do that

JC: Oh wait, I'm sorry, no, he's shooting spots tomorrow morning. He won't be in until maybe late afternoon.

BB: Shooting spots?

JC: LOL, sorry, commercials. He shoots them every week. Would you like to set up an appointment for Thursday?

BB: He shoots them there at the dealership?

JC: Oh no, it's much too busy here. They shoot downtown at Townsend Media. But it really takes all day, so how about I put you in for Thursday? Morning or afternoon?

BB: You know, let me figure out my schedule and I'll get back to you

JC: Alright, Mr. Buckleberry. If you could just answer a short survey...

I clicked out of the chat. And clicked out of the box that asked if I wanted a copy of the chat sent to my email. Jennifer C. would just have to wonder if she truly provided me five-star service.

If shooting their commercials took all day, I assumed they'd start between 8 and 9 am, which meant I should be at Townsend Media by 7:30 or so. I'd get a good night's sleep next to warm Patrick, then come back to the office at 6:30 for coffee and jog downtown with plenty of time to spare. I wasn't sure if the King of Cadillacs had anything to do with this whole thing, but it wouldn't hurt to see Dale Sharpe out of his comfort zone. If looking at his commercials told me anything, it was that Mr. Sharpe presented a false face to the world. Now, it was time to look under the mask.

CHAPTER 6

Townsend Media

It was getting dark, though the snow reflected the last of the dying daylight and lit the forest orange. I stood on my hind legs and pawed at Room 12 of the Highland Motel. The door opened.

"There you are, you little rascal! Where have you been?" asked Mrs. Shaw. I slid between her legs and ran to the bed, jumping next to Patrick. He was doing his homework, lying on the bed on his stomach, and he jumped up to give me a hug.

"Buck! We were worried about you!" He squeezed me tight, a little *too* tight, but I let him because I kind of felt bad that they were actually worried. I rubbed my face against his.

"Did you have a fun day in the snow?" he asked. I wanted to tell him no, that I was actually researching mid-century automobiles and speaking with car dealerships about potential criminal activity, but I thought that might distract him from his math homework.

"Meow," I said instead. He pulled me to his side and settled down to finish figuring out his fractions.

"Patrick, it's pizza tonight. Dad's bringing it home. I mean, here."
"From Capaldi's?"
"No, honey. Domino's."

"Ugh. Okay."

Though I didn't understand it, my humans preferred the authenticity of a Capaldi's pizza, but I really did like the premium chicken on the Cali Chicken Bacon Ranch from the less expensive option. My tail swished a little in anticipation of a yummy treat later on. I knew that Patrick would sneak me a few pieces.

I took a nap before Detective Shaw arrived with dinner. The pizza, of course, was delicious. While the kids ate and watched TV, Shaw talked in guarded tones with his wife, without divulging much of anything, being careful of what was said. But he said enough. Lev had not been located, though there were some leads they were following up on. Technically, Lev was a free man, so there was little that the CSPD could do. But in between routine police work, each of the department's five officers was doing what they could to locate Luzhkov.

I should take this moment to let you know that I did not think that I was a better detective than Shaw. I did not think that I'd find Luzhkov any faster than the CSPD. But I had a choice. I could sit on the motel bed all day or try to help in my own way. I believe most people think that cats are not helpful. In fact, most believe they are the opposite of helpful, and I'd have to agree in most cases. However, when our humans are in jeopardy, you'd be pleasantly surprised at how involved some feline pets would like to be.

When everyone was fast asleep, I helped myself to some crust. I was thoughtful enough to eat it right out of the box so I wouldn't leave a mess on the floor. I leapt up in the window just to check on the patrol car out front. Everything seemed normal. Tucking myself into the curve of Patrick's legs, I thought about what it must be like for Detective Shaw to know that harm may come to his family. I imagined that would be a horrible feeling. I vowed that tomorrow, I would suspend my practice for a few days, hopefully no longer than a week, so that I could help. That made me feel a little bit better, and resting my head on my paws, I finally fell asleep.

My plan was to get a good night's rest, get up early, and meow at the door at 6:30. But Catherine was busy with the kids and rudely ignored my pleas. So I was forced to sneak out when Catherine opened the door closer to 7 to check on the cops in the squad car. That would put me downtown at roughly 7:20 if I didn't stop at the office for coffee. Which immediately put me in a bad mood. I'd have to go straight to town to stake out Townsend Media on Back Street, and then afterward, maybe swing past CSPD to see Tabitha. My tail fluttered.

The jog into town started off cold, but I quickly got used to it. I came up over the ridge at the edge of Red Barn Christmas Tree Farm and sat on an old stump to rest for a moment and look out over the town.

Copper Summit was beautiful, even when there wasn't snow. But in the winter, it became magical. As the sun rose over Mt. Medallion, it illuminated the surrounding mountains behind, creating that beautiful copper color the town was named for. The sunrise bounced off the snow, ice, and rock, making everything around the town shine like a new penny.

After licking a bit of snow from my paws, I hopped down and made my way toward Back Street.

The words had been stenciled into two huge glass windows to either side of the old wooden front door:

TOWNSEND MEDIA
AUDIO • VIDEO • WEB SERVICES

I cleared out some snow and sat across the street underneath the cover of a low rhododendron bush. The clock in the town square had just struck 7:30, so I figured I might as well get comfortable and gathered some leaves to lay on. I was going to be here for a while.

So far, all I saw were people heading into Cool Beans empty-handed, then heading out, their hands wrapped around a warm cup of coffee. Coffee would hit the spot right now. They made a very good dark brew, but unfortunately, I couldn't afford to leave my post. I settled in, burrowing into the leaves a bit to make them more comfortable.

"Well, hey there, mister," said a sultry voice behind me. I turned my head.

"Tabitha," I said. "I was going to visit you later…"

"After your big stakeout?" She had a sly smile on her lips. As the official CSPD cat, she could see right through anything and anyone. She was an attractive tabby, but what made her stand out were the thick, dark markings around her eyes. She looked like she could star in a Disney movie.

I chuckled. "Well, I'm just, I'm just waiting for them to open."

"And then what?"

"Then... I'm going to sneak in."

"I see. Sounds completely above board."

"I don't think it's illegal, as long as they're open," I replied, just a bit worried.

"You dumb cat, I'm joking with you." She nudged me aside and settled into her own soft spot in the leaves next to me. She looked out across the street. "So, what do we have here?"

I could trust her. "You know the Russian guy that just got off? Maybe mob related?"

"Lev Luzhkov. Your owner's in his crosshairs."

"Exactly. I think I saw him last night. I mean, maybe. Someone, at least, was keeping an eye on our motel room. Looked like maybe it was him. And... he was driving an old classic Cadillac."

"So. You're staking out a video production facility. Smart."

"No, no. The King of Cadillacs is shooting commercials there today, so I thought I'd drop in."

"Dale Sharpe? Why not just visit the dealership?"

"I thought I might learn something if he was, you know, out of his element."

"See? Now that is smart thinking. Gonna grill him? Rough him up?"

I turned my head to stare at her. "No."

"Why not? I bet you look good in action."

"The point is not to be seen..."

"Gosh, you really are dumb for a detective. I'm kidding with you. After you nail this guy to the wall, come by the station. I'll have coffee."

"Okay, I..." But she was already up on her haunches, climbing out from under the bush.

"Good luck, hotshot," she said and trotted back to the station.

CHAPTER 7

Studio

Exactly one hour had passed. Just before the clock struck 8:30, an old red pick-up pulled into a spot a few doors down. An average-sized man in a brown Carhartt jacket and jeans stepped out, pulled a briefcase from behind his seat, and locked the truck. He walked to the front door, unlocked it, and stepped inside as the high-pitched bell above the door jingled. He flipped the sign from CLOSED to OPEN.

Over the next twenty minutes or so, three others — two men and one woman — stepped through the doorway. And then, precisely at 9 am, I saw him.

Dale Sharpe walked out of an alleyway beside the building with a huge hulk of a man alongside him. The two could not have been more dissimilar. Dale was thin and bird-like, wearing a bright red puffy winter jacket that was overstuffed with down. The man he walked with weighed twice as much as Dale, thick and muscled, even in his neck. His black peacoat seemed ready to give out at the seams as it tried to contain his bulk. The big man looked both ways as they came from the alley. Dale entered first, bell jangling. Dale did not speak but stepped through, and the large man closed the old door behind him with a bang.

I looked both ways for traffic, then crossed the street. I wasn't getting in through the front door, but there had to be another way in. Sniffing around the edges of the building, I detected the smell of mouse. Cats are much bigger than mice, yes, but cats are also pretty amazing at fitting into tight spaces. Maybe if a mouse found his way in, I could too.

The scent continued around the front of the building, but I didn't see any cracks or openings I could slide through. Once I turned the corner into the alleyway, I noticed two basement windows. The first one, hinged at the top, was locked. The second hung open just a bit and swayed in the breeze. I quickly slipped through.

Landing on a shelf with paint cans, I sat and let my eyes adjust to the dimness of the cellar. It was relatively clean. Nothing was remarkable, just shelves, cardboard boxes, and a large HVAC system in the corner. It hummed as it pumped heat to the upstairs floors.

I hopped down and made my way to the bottom of the wooden steps. Looking up at the closed door, I could hear voices upstairs but couldn't make out the words. Laughter. One by one, I pawed my way up the steps as quietly as possible. More laughter.

The door was slightly ajar, and I peeked out, pulling my whiskers and ears back to keep a low profile. One of the benefits of being a black cat is the ability to blend into the shadows. I learned this the hard way at home, getting stepped on regularly. I always had to be careful where I chose to sit or lay down. Peering around the edge of the door, I felt pretty sure I was as good as invisible.

"...so she hands me her license and says, 'Look, it says it right there, legally blind.' I don't even know how this broad got here, you know?" It's Dale talking. More laughter. "So I say, 'Lady, you can't operate a motor vehicle! How do you expect me to sell you a car? You got a seeing-eye dog that can drive?'" Everyone is laughing except the big guy in black. He stood there, arms in front of him, eyes shifting from side to side. "So she says, 'No, no, I'm not gonna drive it.' I said, 'What?' And she says, 'I just wanna put it in my driveway so it doesn't look like nobody's home!'"

While everyone was laughing, I headed down the hallway, searching for some sort of studio where they'd be shooting the commercials. I needed to find a place to hide before they got started. The floor creaked ahead of me, and I ran for cover into the only open doorway, lifting my tail so it wouldn't be seen. It was the woman who had come in earlier, with long blonde hair, professionally dressed in a satin blouse and tan pants. She walked by the open door carrying a folder stuffed with papers. I didn't know who she was, but she wasn't laughing.

Once she passed, I slipped out of the room and continued my search, finding my way to a large opening at the end of the hall. It wasn't a room but more of a very large open space. The second story had been taken out, so the ceiling was 20 feet high. Almost as high as the ceiling was a lighting grid, with a number of large, black lights placed at odd angles. A curved bright green wall stretched from one side of the back wall to the other, almost forming a semicircle. A camera on a thick tripod was set up in the middle of the studio, with a cable connected to a large monitor. Nothing was powered on yet, just the fluorescents high above. In the corner, there were a half dozen cylindrical lights made of black metal that were piled on the floor. I squeezed between a few of them and turned around. My view of the studio was perfect, and in this darkened corner, I wouldn't be noticed. No sooner had I settled in when I heard voices coming down the hall.

I peered over the edge of one of the big lights.

The man who opened the shop was speaking. This must be Mr. Townsend.

"Looks like we've got ten today. You got this," said the man. Dale exhaled as they walked into the studio. "At least it's not 13. That was a day."

"Yeah," Dale uttered softly, not nearly as animated as he was five minutes prior. I ducked back down.

"Okay, you know your spot, let's hit it. Alan, can you get him mic'd up?"

Dale moved to a mark on the floor, just a line of tape. As he adjusted his suit jacket, Alan, the younger guy in a dark polo and khakis, put a lapel microphone on him. Alan hid the wire inside the suit jacket, taping it in place.

"What are we thinking for lunch?" Dale asked. "I don't want that Asian stuff we had last time. What was the name of that place? Chickpea?"

"Chen Pai, " said Alan as he straightened Dale's suit jacket.

"Right. We need good Chinese in this town."

"Jim'll bring in the menus once we get a few spots down. You already hungry for lunch?"

"Just thinking ahead."

Alan was done with the mic placement and went behind the camera, powering it on. The HD monitor lit up. Jim, presumably the other production assistant, pushed some levers on a large panel, and all the lights above slowly came to life. The green wall became so bright it was almost blinding.

A box about the size of a laptop sat on rails in front of the camera lens. Jim moved from the lighting panel to the camera and adjusted a few things to the box. He asked Dale if he could see the text.

"Looking good," he said, giving a thumbs up.

So, the script was put onto a two-way mirror in front of the lens, and that was how Dale read his lines. Human technology was amazing. He whispered through the script several times as it rolled up the screen.

The woman who almost caught me in the hallway was seated in the back of the studio, watching the proceedings, legs crossed. She dangled her foot impatiently. She, and the big guy, were the only ones I couldn't rightfully place. Was she an assistant? Did she work for Townsend Media or Dale Sharpe Cadillac? She almost seemed a little too refined to work for Dale.

The big guy was in the back as well and stood with his arms in front of him, one hand holding the other wrist. He'd taken off his black coat, and his muscles bulged under his black turtleneck.

"Mr. Sharp? Could you look toward the camera, please?" Jim asked. Dale turned his body, smoothed his thinning hair, and put on his best smile. Jim made some camera adjustments, and Mr. Townsend stepped behind him, looking over his shoulder. Then, Townsend stepped in front of the larger HD monitor, crossed his arms, and set himself in place, ready to start shooting.

"How we doing, Dale? Ready?" he asked. "Start rolling, Jim, please." Jim pressed a red button on the side of the camera.

"Let's do it," Dale said.

"Alright. In three, two, one…"

CHAPTER 8

Action

Townsend shot him a finger, indicating he could start speaking at any time. It took a moment, but eventually, after a few swallows, Dale started to speak to the camera.

"It's, ah, me, Dale Sharpe, Cad of Kingalacs… ahhhh darn."

"It's okay, it's okay, we'll take it right from the top. Ready?" Townsend asked.

Dale cleared his throat, nodded his head, and began again. "It's me, Dale Sharpe, King of Cadillacs and we have a Cadillac, offer, an offer for you…" He shook his head and apologized, exercising his mouth and tongue. Was this what all of the commercial shoots were like? How did they possibly get them all done in one day? I turned around a few times between the jumble of lights I was hiding within and then laid down to get comfortable. I might be here a while.

"Let's just get the first line and move on to the second. Good?"

Dale nodded. He looked over to the thug in black, exhaling and wiping some sweat from his brow. He chuckled a bit. "I… I'll get it."

"Can we just pat him down a bit?" Townsend asked either Jim or Alan, whoever could respond first. Alan grabbed a small makeup compact from a workbench and, stepping up to Dale, he applied a small amount of powder to his shining forehead. Alan looked back at Townsend, who gave a thumbs-up approval. "Alright, Dale, from the top."

I looked over to Thug. From my vantage point slightly behind him, I saw the bulge in the small of his back under the black ribbed turtleneck. He was definitely carrying. Now, why would Dale need protection like that? Especially here in Copper Summit? Was that what Thug was? Protection?

"Hey, it's Dale Sharpe, King of Cadillacs, and check out this offer!" He delivered the line neatly, without stumbling. Townsend clapped his hands once.

"That's the one. Nice job. Mark that one, Jim. Let's move on to the next."

Thug stood as still as the clock in town square. In his turtleneck. Which made me think of Mr. Tuttle, the turtle with the missing house. Could someone really have stolen his entire house? That seemed absurd. But Mr. Tuttle did seem a bit... odd. Maybe, instead of thinking that someone stole his house, could he just have, maybe, forgotten where he lived? He did seem older. Though turtles lived a long time, didn't they?

Dale Sharpe went through take after take of his lines, stumbling, stuttering, always looking over to Thug when he broke eye contact with the camera lens, almost like he was afraid there'd be some retribution if he kept making mistakes. Sharpe did his best to plow through the scripts, and when he finally completed three, Townsend asked Jim to go get the folder of menus.

"What do we feel like today?" Townsend said to the room. "Dale? Chinese?"

"Funny. No, not today. Pizza sound good?" That got approval from everyone.

"Alright then, let's take a break, and we'll let these lights cool down."

After Alan dimmed and powered down the lighting grid in the ceiling, everyone started to file out of the studio and back to the main reception room, where there were couches and chairs to sit in while waiting for lunch to arrive. I raised my head a bit so my ears stuck out above the lights. But Thug stayed back and stopped Dale as the rest of the group left. Lowering my head again, I watched. Footsteps and voices echoed down the hall. He placed a hand on Dale's chest.

"This foolishness. It stops." So. He had a Russian accent.

"I, I know, it's just, it's not easy! You try it!"

He chuckled. "People, they do not want me selling them cars," Thug said slowly. "They think there's body in trunk."

"Yeah. You have a point. I'm trying, alright?" Dale lowered his voice and looked towards the hallway. "Like, this is not my *forte* you know?"

"Yes, this I know."

"Face-to-face, I can sell the Pope crack. Once I look into that camera…"

"You become skittish. Like the hare. Running away." He made a running motion with his fingers.

"Well, Toli, I don't know about that…"

"You finish. Then, we go and talk about Lev and son." So, Lev has a son?

Dale cleared his throat. "Sounds like a plan."

So, Thug's name was Toli? Anatoli? And he knew about Lev?

The big Russian stepped up to him, inches away from his face. Dale had to tilt his head up. He tapped Dale's head with his fat finger.

"Use this, yes? Your brain." He brought his hand back down. "Be the battleship."

Dale looked at him, confused.

"The battleship. Strong. Moving forward."

"Ah. Yes. That's, that's good advice actually."

"Now, we eat." He clapped Dale hard on the back, hard enough to make him cough.

On their way out of the studio, Dale asked, "What do you like on your pizza?"

Toli kept moving forward, not looking back as Dale followed.

"Hare," he said.

CHAPTER 9

CSPD Coffee Break

The entryway to Copper Summit Police Station was a double set of automatic glass doors, allowing me a paws-free entrance. Getting into the station was easier than going through my cat door at home.

Tabitha was there waiting for me in the station lobby, and Mary, the portly Desk Sargeant, leaned over her counter and said, "Well, hello, Mr. Buckleberry. Good to see you again." I smiled up at her.

Tabitha took me into the break room. Having Tabitha as the station cat was never a problem. Officer Amy Fordham had rescued her about a year ago and everyone there loved her. But when I came to visit, even though I belonged to Shaw, some officers thought it was problematic, at best. Mary didn't think so. But thankfully, everything was mostly quiet at CSPD, and we were relatively safe from discovery. I followed her between two vending machines.

"So?" she asked.

"You said there would be coffee."

"Ah. Yes. Stay here."

I watched her as she jumped onto the counter to retrieve two small yellow Dixie cups. Taking one gently in her mouth, she carefully climbed down a series of cardboard boxes and placed it in front of me. Then she went back to get hers, repeating the process. We nosed our coffee cups along and slid under the snack machine. No one could see us, which meant no one could shoo us out from here.

Dixie cups are not famous for retaining heat. The coffee was cold but good. If there's one thing I hate, it's a lukewarm cup of coffee. Scalding is fine. Cold is fine. Anything else, no thanks. For me, it was perfect, and I told Tabitha so.

"Well, thank you, Mr. Buckleberry. But I didn't make it. I stole it."

"The good thing is, if they put you in jail for it, you can just slip right through the bars."

"They'll have to catch me first." She winked.

I told her what happened at the studio, how nervous Dale was around the bodyguard or whatever he was, and the conversation I overheard after everyone else had left.

"Has anyone by the name Anatoli ever been mentioned around here?" I asked.

"Hmm, not that I recall. I can look through a few things, I guess, and see what I come up with."

"He's huge, maybe 6'5", 250, I'm guessing. Short blond hair, like buzzed short. Definitely Eastern European. I want to say Russian, but what's Russia anymore? Could have been Balkan, Armenian. I don't know." I lapped at my coffee.

"You know," I said, after a few sips, "you can always come by my office for a coffee, too. I've got an amazing Kona blend."

"Is that so?" she asked.

"That is so. Though until the Shaws get back to a normal routine, my office hours are hit and miss."

"Like your detective work?"

I gave her a sidelong glance. "You think you could check out this Anatoli guy for me?"

"The station is pretty desolate after midnight. I'll see what I can find on NCIC as soon as I get the chance. Typically, two officers are out on patrol, and one stays here, along with a dispatcher. But sometimes people get changed around or called out, and then the station's mine."

NCIC was the National Crime Information Center, and I was sure Anatoli would turn up in it somewhere. There was some noise just outside the door, talking and footsteps, which eventually worked their way into the break room. We both eased back a little further under the vending machine. I saw two pairs of standard police-issue black duty boots. They made their way towards the coffee machine.

"It's not that bad. Two beds, a television, what more do you need?"

"I know, Will, but being away from your house. Kinda sucks."

The clink of the carafe being taken out. Liquid poured. Stirring.

"Agreed. We'll be back soon. Rogers told me earlier that they'd seen him heading toward the state line this morning. They've got eyes out all around the county. Also, let the VA Staties know about him, so hopefully, we hear something soon."

"That's Detective Shaw," I whispered to Tabitha.

"Thanks, Sherlock, I see him every day," she whispered.

"Let me know if Emma and I can do anything," said Alvarez. "You guys good with dinners?"

"Dinner? What's that?" They both laughed. "It's only been two days, but Catherine's about ready to kill me. Maybe we give it another day or two and then just come on back."

"Uh-huh. Well, the State Police won't be keeping an eye on your place for much longer, you know. They've got better things to do."

"Exactly. Maybe I tell Catherine we're all clear. Head back tonight. Beat the snow."

"*If* it comes. They were wrong last time."

"They usually are."

They continued talking on their way out of the break room, and after a moment or two, I could no longer hear what they were saying. Tabitha and I could speak freely again.

"You think it's safe?" I asked her.

"According to what I read in the records and incident logs, no."

"I think I agree with you."

"So what are you going to do, Buck?"

"Stake out the house on my own. And drink a lot of coffee."

CHAPTER 10

Catnip & Crooks

Before I left CSPD, I heard dispatch call the NC State Highway Patrol to go ahead and pull that car from Copper Summit. I'm sure Detective Shaw wouldn't enjoy the conversation he was about to have with his wife later today, though she might be happy to have her house back.

I ambled through the woods that connected the town with the street I lived on.

Detective Shaw had numerous reports that the Cadillac was last seen on its way into Virginia, but nothing more since that last report. He and the other cops thought he was safe. I disagreed. Why would they assume the danger had passed? The only thing I could think was that one, they couldn't be sure that it was indeed Lev Luzhkov driving said vehicle, and two, nor could they be sure that said vehicle came from Dale Sharpe's lot. That had to be their reasoning. Also, since his release, Lev had not been seen by anyone, neither cop nor citizen. Therefore, they had nothing to go on and certainly nothing substantial that would hold up should this whole matter go to court.

I, however, could connect at least a few dots. From the conversation in the studio, Lev was certainly on the radar of Dale Sharpe and his protective gorilla, Toli. Not only was Lev known by them, but apparently, his son was too. Organized crime was a family business, whether that was in North Carolina or the outer stretches of Siberia.

As a detective, I have two laws concerning my work. The second is, always leave time for lunch. But the first is, never assume.

The Shaw's house came into sight through the dense forest, and I slowed my pace. It was only midafternoon, but the setting sun shone almost horizontally through the blowing boughs and branches. It was getting cooler, too. I padded up to my office door, opened it and stepped inside. The smell of cedar and pine, an always welcome scent, greeted me. It was cold, so I went to the fireplace and put some kindling on the grate (in this case, the shredded cardboard packaging from the Creamy Vittles® case I dragged to my office from the house). With a long match, I set it ablaze. A few pine branches on top of that, and it was already getting toasty.

Tea. That's what I needed. Taking down a mug from the cupboard, I dropped a bag of Earl Grey into it, then pulled out one of the porcelain canisters in which I kept the catnip. Today was a double-scoop kind of day. I set the water to boil on the small stove.

Back in the office, I pulled a Q-Tip from the stash next to an overstuffed chair, settled onto the small rug in front of the fire, and started playing with it. Something about batting one of these things around helped me think clearly. Or occasionally biting the hard center stick. Maybe sometimes taking it in my front paws and scraping off all the cotton with my back ones. That was especially satisfying.

So, Lev Luzhkov escapes from Siberia. From prison? I don't know. Who voluntarily lives in Siberia? He then overpowers (did that mean kill?) three fishermen and commandeers their vessel. Makes it to shore in Alaska. Somehow travels thousands of miles to the other side of the country. For what?

Wait a minute... not for what. For who. Anatoli had mentioned that he and Dale would talk about Lev and his son. Was Luzhkov's son here in North Carolina? But before he could meet up with him...

A loud shriek filled the room. I jumped up, wild-eyed, suddenly on all fours, looking around before realizing it was the tea kettle. As I turned off the burner, my pupils slowly shrank to normal size.

I understand that most cats like English Breakfast. However, I've found that catnip blends much better with Earl Grey, and now I won't even consider anything else with my nip.

Tea poured, I sat in my comfy chair by the fire and sipped. Ah, how I could speak endlessly of the splendors of tea and nip combined. For those not of the feline persuasion, how do I even put into words the gentle combination of the two? The swirl of loose *Nepeta cataria* caught within a fragrant whirlpool of stimulant and sedation — coexisting, one feeding off the other until you feel like you could simultaneously fall into a dream or bite the arm of your chair to shreds...

The cup was half empty, and I managed to place it on the hearth, curling and turning in the chair until I decided the best position was belly up, with all four paws up in the air. If only the most royal of kings had such sophistication and contentment. My eyes closed, and purring, I fell asleep.

I don't know how much time had passed, but it was dark outside, and the fire had gone out. Something was itching my face. I shook my head and pawed at it. What was that? I woke up fully.

Sitting up on my haunches, I rubbed my face again and licked my paw. Was that… sawdust? I looked up. Indeed, sawdust fell from above me. I jumped down from the chair and looked at the ceiling.

Now I could hear footsteps. Someone was up above me in the shed, moving quietly. Wherever they stepped, dust fell through the cracks. Was it Mr. Shaw looking for a shovel, perhaps? I shook the rest of the catnip cobwebs from my mind and climbed up the shelves into the corner where there was a small gap between the ceiling of my office and the floor of the shed above. It was unusual for Shaw to rummage through the shed in the dark. Something didn't feel right.

There, through a tiny quarter-inch crack, was the biggest man I had ever seen. Lev Luzhkov.

55

PART TWO
SNOWSTORM

CHAPTER 11

Going For A Ride

My ears instinctively pushed themselves back on my head, lowering my profile, although there was no way he could see me. He was a beast of a man, wearing dirty work boots and dark blue coveralls. He held a small flashlight in his mouth as he looked around, illuminating the lawn equipment and shelves filled with boxes and junk. It also lit up his features from underneath, making him look grisly and grotesque. I remembered his face from the police reports, fat but chiseled. Ugly. Small eyes that reminded me of the tiny laser that Patrick would sometimes play with in his room that would get me unhinged for a few short minutes. Because those eyes could shoot lasers from them, especially if, say, you had put him in prison for three years.

He held a can of beer that looked miniature in his grasp. He turned and rummaged through some shelves for a few moments, being careful not to make any sound. Then he turned back.

He wiped his thick hands on his coveralls and looked around the dark shed with the tiny flashlight, then approached the closed double doors and looked through the gap. He grunted. From here, he could see the back of the Shaw's house, lights on in the kitchen, and one more in Patrick's room. This wasn't good.

Lev slowly lifted the latch from the inside and stepped out into the winter night.

I quietly scrambled down and went to a long horizontal window set high up in my office, putting my front paws on the sill. Above the window, there was a few feet of overhang from the floor of the shed, but I could still see relatively clearly. Lev's boots took up most of my vision. It seemed like he was deciding whether or not to approach the house.

Sparks fell. No, not sparks, but lit ashes. Lev had lit up a cigarette. He stood there for a few moments in the dark, contemplating who knows what, and then stepped away from the shed and away from the house. I quickly went to the office door and slipped out, closing it softly. Slinking around the back of the shed, I saw Lev walking into the woods, away from the house, his cigarette leaving a red ghostly glow in his hand.

He was easy to follow, and I kept about 20 yards behind him as he trudged through the snow. It wasn't that deep and had a thin veneer of ice on top, so it cracked with every step he took. That hid what little sound I made as I padded along behind him, stopping when he did, hiding in bushes or behind trees when I was able. My black fur against the white snow wasn't ideal. But at least it was night.

He moved through the woods with a purposeful stride, and with every step he took, I was thankful that it was in the opposite direction of the Shaw's house. I only wished that someone knew what I was doing, where I was going. I had a feeling that this was not going to end well. But what was I to do? My family was in danger, and I was the only one who knew about it. I had to follow him.

Eventually, there was a clearing in the woods. Oakridge Lane cut through the forest at that point, about a half mile away from the Shaw house. And sitting there on the side of the road was the Coupe DeVille. I hid behind a tree as Lev unlocked the driver's door and opened it. Then, after a moment of thought, he walked around the front of the car, walked up to a tree, and unzipped.

It was now or never. I ran behind the car, around the side, and slipped through the driver's door, hiding under the front seat. My heart pounded. What was I doing?

I was protecting my family.

Lev opened the door a little more to make room for his wide bulk, and then, with a creak, the door slammed shut. The engine started, and I curled myself into the smallest ball possible.

I was either brave from the lingering effects of the catnip or brave because I loved my family. I like to think it was the latter.

The car pulled away from the curb.

CHAPTER 12

Road Trip

The space under the passenger seat was surprisingly clean, spotless even. The maroon carpet made it warm, and the heater blew fresh air over me. This was the only consolation of being trapped in a murderer's vehicle on his way to who knew where. As we turned the corner at the stop sign at the end of Oakridge, I heard a metallic clink next to me. In the passing streetlight, I saw it. The glint of a long steel blade, a fisherman's tool, I thought, long and narrow and serrated on the edge. A filet knife.

I moved away from it, fearing that maybe on the next turn it would tumble and cut me. But as soon as I moved, I heard Lev grunt as his hand reached underneath the seat, fat fingers looking for the knife. He touched my fur, and I jumped forward. The car swayed as his eyes left the road, but he didn't seem to react to feeling my thick black coat. I quietly crawled to the back, and his hand finally found the hilt, pulling it from under the bench and placing it next to him. He turned on the radio.

In a car this old, I figured there was only an AM band. He punched some of the buttons on the ancient radio, and it went from news talk to gospel. Gospel to country. Country to oldies, which is finally what he settled on. I recognized the song. *Sleepwalk* by Santo and Johnny. At least this killer had good taste in music.

The ride was so smooth it barely felt like we were moving. If I had ever been in a boat, I would think that this is what it would be like; soft, fluid motions, slow and easy, like rocking a baby to sleep.

I chanced hopping up onto the back seat, thinking that if I were directly behind him, there'd be no way he could see me, short of stopping the car and turning around. The leather was a cream color like the exterior but had maroon trim that matched the carpet. The seat was soft on my paws.

Bare trees filtered the moonlight as I looked up. I figured by now we were at least a mile away from home, heading away from town. I put my paws on the side window and looked out. The only thing out this way was forest, rock outcroppings, and curves that you couldn't take at more than 30mph, or you'd flip. I'd seen a few accidents on this stretch of road, mostly in the winter and mostly by people who'd never traveled them before. Out-of-towners. The locals did not like out-of-towners.

There were occasional houses set back into the woods, lights on, fires lit. The next town up was Pearl Lake. But the only thing in Pearl Lake was… well, Pearl Lake. I wasn't sure what exactly Lev was driving towards. There was literally nothing in this direction unless you drove almost an hour to I-81. And I hoped he wasn't going to do that, or I might never see my family again.

Just to be safe, I jumped down onto the floorboard and curled up in a ball behind Lev's seat. Maybe this wasn't the best idea.

Eventually, the car slowed. I saw the trees light up red outside the window as he applied the brakes. I jumped up to the window again to see exactly where we were.

The middle of nowhere.

But there was a road. Dirt, but a road nonetheless. He turned onto it.

The shocks on this car were amazing. The road was filled with potholes and trenches and ruts the size of sewer pipes, but the Coupe handled everything with ease. I looked forward over Lev's shoulder and saw only the deepest, darkest forest. The headlights could only illuminate so far, and then, blackness. Trees, rocks, dirt. That's all there was. I scrambled to the floor and hid again under the passenger side of the front seat. Lev stopped the car.

The door opened. He kept the car running.

Cold seeped into the car, even with the heat on. Inch by inch, I stuck my head out from underneath the seat, realizing that my ears would give me away first. I had to see what was happening. But there was nothing, just the open door and the faintly illuminated trees beyond the door. I crept out from underneath to get a better look.

There was not much to see from the open door, so I stretched out to the dashboard.

Lev stood at the front of the car, arms crossed with his back to me, dark coveralls illuminated by the headlights. And then, as if on cue, someone stepped out from the woods. Short blond hair, gaunt face. Jeans, work boots, and a dark jacket with some kind of insignia on the chest. He walked up to Lev. Words were exchanged in what I had to assume was Russian. A pause, and then the two hugged each other as if they hadn't seen each other in years.

After a short embrace, Lev held the younger man by his shoulders, pushing him away, looking at him, laughing, then pulling him close again. More talking from Lev, animated. Lev stepped back. It seemed the younger man did not know much Russian, and Lev did not know much English. But somehow, they communicated.

He and the young man talked back and forth for a while, and then the young man took his finger and traced something on his hand. Like he was drawing something for Lev. He made sure Lev was paying attention.

After a few minutes, Lev hugged the younger man again and pointed at him, saying something over and over. I figured this was my time to leave the car, so I hopped onto the seat and then onto the floor, making my way to the open door. But dark overalls blocked my exit. I hopped back into the car and, panicking, jumped over the seat. Lev saw me. He grabbed the knife.

"Aveenya!" he yelled.

I moved to the rear window, hissing, as Lev shoved the sharp knife toward me. Baring my teeth, I let out a low growl and swiped with my paw, claws out. He shouted again, and as he swung the knife towards me, I ducked under it, skittering under the driver's seat and out the door before he ever knew what had happened. I was out of the car in under a second, my heart beating faster than it ever had. I ran until I could hide behind a rock a dozen yards away, then risked a look back.

Lev raised his voice to the younger man, yelling and waving his fisherman's knife. But thirty seconds or so later, they were both laughing, and the younger man turned towards me briefly. I could see the insignia on his jacket in the Coupe's headlights.

Dale Sharpe, King of Cadillacs.

CHAPTER 13

Dark Forest

There was no one left after the red glow of the Cadillac's tail lights disappeared down the forest pathway. The man, who must have been Lev's son, was also gone, walking away into the darkness in the opposite direction until I heard nothing but far-away crunches in the dry leaves. And then, silence.

I was not sure of the time, but the sky was brightening on the horizon, though the trees and brush hid most of it. I was disoriented but not completely lost. I knew that if I followed the trail back to the main road, all I had to do was turn right, make one left onto an unmarked road, and I'd eventually come back to the Shaw's. But I had no idea how long it would take. I started on my way.

The trail was mostly cleared of snow, probably because the tree cover here was so thick, and there was less chance of accumulation. I kept to the dirt parts to keep my paws warmer. At least the sun was coming up.

Turning my head to see how long until sunrise, something odd caught my eyes. A letter, or maybe a symbol, was carved into a birch tree. I turned around and walked up to the old white tree.

About six feet up was a deep gouge in the bark, in what looked like a lowercase 'p', but not quite. Extending my claws, I hopped up against the trunk, clawing my way up to the symbol. I pawed some of the snow and ice away to better inspect it. This wasn't any letter I'd seen before. I sniffed at it. Must have been old because all I could sense was the tea-like quality of birch bark. The best way to describe this odd-looking symbol would be as a 'p' with a curlicue running through the end... a pig's tail.

Were there other trees like this one? Hopping down to the forest floor, I sat at the base, waiting for the sun to illuminate the trees just a little.

I'd mentioned earlier about two laws concerning my work. Well, there was a third: exercise patience.

While my eyes adjusted to the forest around me, I scanned the trees for another symbol. Just as my eyes began to tire, I saw it — another one on a tree about twenty yards away. I quickly hopped in that direction, and as I approached the next pigtail, I could plainly see another up ahead.

It took close to thirty minutes before I came to the end of the pigtail trail.

This tree stood next to the mouth of a cave, hidden with moss that hung from rocks above. Was this where Lev's son had come from?

I paced back and forth in front of the entrance to the cave, tail flicking, wondering what might be inside, wondering if something or someone lived there, wondering if I somehow became trapped, would I ever escape.

And then I thought about the Shaws. Any one of them could be in danger. There was so much I didn't know. But this cave, maybe it held a clue for me. I was sure that's where Lev's son (admittedly, that was a guess) had come from. So... what was at the other end?

I stepped to the cave's wide opening, onto soft moss that led into a broad passage. All I could see were rock walls supported by occasional beams and rafters. So it was more of a tunnel. There were sporadic bulbs above, but none were lit. I couldn't help myself. Curiosity had gotten the better of me. I stepped in.

There was an old wooden box set into the rock wall to the right. A large rusted metal handle was set into the box, in the down position.

The fur on my spine bristled. I had to force myself to keep moving forward. Although it felt warmer in here by a few degrees, a slight, damp breeze flowed over me, and in the distance, a low, hollow howl never stopped. I looked behind me.

As a deep orange filled the hole of the cavern opening, the sunrise behind the trees, there was nothing but darkness ahead of me.

I tried to move forward, but it became so dark that my eyes could no longer discern anything ahead. The bank of bare bulbs above snapped on. The walls and support beams were suddenly illuminated in harsh yellow light, and voices came from the other end of the tunnel. I froze.

I scurried behind a rafter, jumping up into a crevice between the old wood and the cold rock, and pushed myself back. But trying to fit into the small crack, I saw another larger one above me, next to a support beam that held up the ceiling. I climbed up the wood and made my body flush with the small seam so that only my head was looking out and down onto the tunnel floor. Even with a flashlight, I didn't think whoever it was that was coming would see me up here. I waited.

The voices became clearer. And now I could determine that they were coming from the mouth of the cave. If I had turned around ten minutes earlier, I would have been discovered. The talking ceased for the moment, and something dragged in the dirt. A shuffling of feet. The soft grunts and groans of a pair of men struggling with something. Then, shadows along the far cave wall. The men were almost here.

I shrank back further.

Two large men came into view. Tan coveralls, ball caps. In the seconds that it took for them to pass under me, I could not identify them. Between the two of them, one man walking forward, the other backward, was a man draped between them. Hanging. Most likely dead, with a harsh wound to the side of the skull. I only saw it for an instant before the face was covered in shadows, but the wound looked deep. And perfectly round. One of the men said, "There's got to be an easier way." The other man grunted.

I peered around the old rafter as they got farther and farther away until they rounded another corner. It was safe to jump down.

I had a choice about what to do next. Go forward into the tunnel. Or go back to the safety of home. But I knew I couldn't do that, wouldn't do that. If I had a chance to protect my family, I had to take that chance.

Leaving behind the sunlight and safety of the cave entrance, I walked the other way, following the little smears of blood on the ground, into the depths of the dark cave, the wind howling softly like a ghost.

CHAPTER 14

Tunnel

Let me assure you of something: Cats do not have more than one life. I've known plenty of feline friends over the years who did not reach their allotted nine. That made me thankful that I was no longer an outdoor cat. There are so many dangers, toils, and snares in that kind of life. Like finding oneself in an underground cave following two criminals and a body. Not much good can come of that.

But I followed far behind. There were enough curves in this tunnel, allowing me to keep my distance, yet still hear the hushed tones of the people up ahead, and the sliding of the corpse.

The overhead bulbs flickered and dimmed occasionally, leaving me wondering if, at some point, they might just give out. I hoped not. I kept moving forward.

Who knew I was here? Absolutely no one. I'd been gone since 10 pm the night before. The Shaws were probably not worried yet. If I missed tonight's dinner, I'm sure they'd start wondering where I was. That was twelve hours away. Tabitha thought I was staking out the house.

I rounded the next corner and found myself at a split in the path, standing at the cross-section of a Y at a standstill.

The lights went out.

My chest tightened, and all my senses went on high alert. My pupils expanded to their maximum, but it still wasn't enough in this subterranean darkness. I crouched down, not knowing what to expect, backing up a few inches, low to the ground, claws extended. My heart raced as I tried to figure out what to do.

Then I heard it, a scraping, like metal against rock. I sat up and turned my ears like tiny satellite dishes, first to the left and then to the right, each in a different direction. Yes, there it was — the tunnel to the right.

I could hear a mouse in the neighbor's bushes from three houses down, so hearing something in the echo chamber of a tunnel wasn't a problem, even if it was far away. But admittedly, I was scared.

Do I turn around? What if the lights never come back?

No. I press on. Something was happening here, and it involved the safety of my family.

I walked in the direction of where I thought the right tunnel entrance would be. My whiskers felt the rock before I walked into it. I started walking forward, slowly down the pathway.

I kept my right side against the rock wall, carefully following it. A good bath was going to be mandatory when I got home. If I did.

The lights blinked on and off and then steadily grew back to a dim illumination. The shuffling sounds and occasional voices were inaudible, now replaced with a low rumble in the air. Not just a rumble I could hear, but one that I felt deep in my chest. There was something powerful up ahead. I could even feel it in the pads of my paws.

Now I was in a very long and straight section of cave, probably fifty yards or so. If someone appeared, I'd be caught and have to run in the opposite direction — there was no place to hide. I jogged the full length of it, feeling and hearing the rumble grow into a roar. I'm not sure if my heart had ever beaten so fast.

I should have left a note on my desk for Ariella to find in case I never made it back. Or a message in an envelope for Tabitha. Anything. I had a bad feeling about this.

The long passage ended with a wide turn to the left. As I peeked around the rocks, the roar became thunder.

At the end, I could see a bright orange circle with cascades of water rushing forcefully down just beyond. The rising sun was burning through a tremendous waterfall, leaving the two men in silhouette as they wrestled with the body. Were they tying something to it?

I risked coming out from around the corner, again staying against the rock wall. I slowly made my way half the distance to the end before deciding that I was close enough. I climbed a rafter and settled in on top, deep in the shadows. Again, the scraping of metal on rock.

Were they zip-tying the man's arms? Was he still alive? I moved my head forward a few inches. No… they were tying something to him. Something heavy. Something metal. Something to keep the body from floating to the surface once it hit the bottom.

It was a rusty flywheel. A large gear-like part of a car. This one looked like it weighed a hundred pounds, flaked with decay, and dripping wet. They tied it in several places with large zip ties and rope. Using the hole in the center to put the rope through, they lassoed his arms, legs, chest, neck. They were careful. They checked their work. I wondered if they'd done this before.

Then they stood, the larger man clapping his hands and wiping them on his pants. With his boot, he kicked the back of the dead man. Without a sound, he rolled over the edge, disappearing. The roar of the water was loud enough that I couldn't hear a splash. They turned and walked toward me, black shadows against the bright orange cascade of water.

"*Do svidaniya*," one of the men said, laughing, as they walked under me.

That was one of the few Russian words I did know.

Goodbye.

CHAPTER 15

Snowstorm

I stayed in place for 10 minutes or so, hoping the men wouldn't return. With the rush of water next to me, there was no way to hear anyone coming from behind. So I waited.

Eventually, I crept down, always looking over my shoulder. I carefully made my way to the edge of the cave.

The sun had risen enough so that the water was no longer orange but a light green. Mist and droplets fell against my fur. I shook it off, stepped to the edge, and looked down. It was a long drop.

I couldn't see the bottom. It was covered in a cloud of water about 100 feet below. I quickly glanced behind me, making sure no one was approaching. I looked back to the waterfall. Where in the world was I? I had no idea a waterfall even existed in Copper Summit.

There was nothing for me to see here. It was either rushing green water or an explosion of vapor far below. I couldn't see the sky; I couldn't see the ground. And there was no way I could walk out onto the cliff. I had no choice. I had to turn around.

Whoever those two men were, they had turned off the lights. I wondered if this was an old abandoned mine shaft from a century before when iron ore was a major export here. Looking ahead, the path eventually became solid darkness. Reluctantly, I started on my way into the black abyss.

Without at least a small amount of existing light from the outside world to heighten my sense of sight, I was blind. Every step I took was slow and deliberate. I was as scared as I'd ever been.

Rats scuttled around me. Maybe mice. In my mind, I pretended they were mice. They avoided me, and once I knew they were past me, I moved forward once again, further into the darkness.

I stayed to the left, always keeping my body in touch with the rock, so when it turned, I turned with it. This made the most sense to me, and I hoped I remembered correctly.

After about a half hour of slinking along the black walls, I was rewarded with a circle of light far, far away. I ran toward the opening. Soon, I could see the branches of trees covered in dense fog.

The closer I came, the more I could see, and eventually, I realized that it wasn't fog that obscured the trees but heavy snow. I stood at the opening, my eyes adjusting to daylight and the sight before me. How long had I been in here?

The wind created a deep howl at the mouth of the cave, and the snow outside was blowing sideways. It looked like maybe three to four inches had already fallen. Without even stepping outside, I realized how cold I was. Unfortunately, I had no idea how far from home I'd come.

Thankfully, I knew how to get back.

I rubbed my face with my paw and shook off the snow that was covering me. I stepped out into the storm.

Make a right. Travel through the birch trees for a few hundred yards. Get to the makeshift road that leads into the forest from the main road. Follow the ruts out to the main road. Make a right again, then follow that road for a bit until I get to the unmarked road where the Shaw's house sits on the left.

I knew what I had to do, and as I trotted along, the snow was getting deeper and deeper. As the storm approached, it was also becoming quite dark. The wind blew my fur up, exposing my skin, feeling like icy needles. I kept the map focused in my mind. If I thought about the cold, or the danger, or anything else, it would slow me down. I thought only of my end goal and did my best to ignore the rest.

Be the battleship, as Toli had said.

As I traveled down the double-rutted path, I heard a heavy panting. It seemed a few hundred yards away, but with the snow dampening all sound, it was probably much closer. I stopped to listen, crouching low to the ground, halfway buried in the fresh snow.

A black cat surrounded by white snow. A perfect target.

My ears pivoted to the left. There it was. Not one, but a pair of some sort of dogs, coyotes, maybe even wolves. Now I heard not just their panting but the trotting through the forest as eight canine pads crushed the snow beneath them, loping toward me. Their stride hadn't paused or quickened, so I figured they had yet to catch my scent. I hoped I was downwind.

I crawled behind the nearest tree, jumping from the snow up onto the white trunk, initially slipping, then sinking my claws into the soft birch. Climbing higher and higher, I finally saw them. A pair of gray-white coyotes.

Tongues hanging out, they ran loosely, stride after stride. Then, they noticed it. The scent of my fear. I dared to climb a little higher, putting more distance between us. They both stopped uncomfortably close to my tree.

Noses high, they sniffed all around them, knowing something was there. Sometimes dogs can be dumb, but coyotes, they're wild animals. And very smart. I sat perfectly still. They put their front paws on the tree in which I sat.

But the snow confused them, carrying my scent with the wind to places I was not. They turned in circles and sniffed at the bases of other trees. But eventually, they knew that whatever they had smelled was either long gone or farther away than they wanted to travel. They looked at each other and started running back along their path.

I relaxed, my back flattening and my ears slowly standing straight again. I watched the pair run into the woods far from the old road. I shook the snow from my fur.

If you've ever been lucky enough to be the caretaker for a cat, then you'll understand that we take multiple naps during the day. Honestly, it's something humans should do as well. But I'd been awake since the previous night and was cold and exhausted. All I needed was a short nap high up in the protection of this tree. Yes, I'd be snowed on, but I wrapped my tail around my body, covered my nose, and settled my paws between thick branches to keep myself secure and somewhat protected from the worst of the wind. I shivered and curled into a tighter ball. Eventually, I fell asleep.

My nap could have been thirty minutes or three hours. All I knew was that it was still snowing when I woke, but I felt a little more rested. I shook myself clean.

Getting down was a challenge. The branches and bark were slippery from the snow. I moved cautiously, and after a few minutes, I made my final hop to the ground. Certain that the coyotes were far away by now, I continued along the path. Before long, I heard the occasional car hissing from the main road and I knew I was closer to home.

The snow had not let up at all, and the pads of my paws were freezing. I sat down in a hollow next to a tree and brought my back paws up to my mouth, one at a time, chewing away the snow and ice that had frozen between my pads. It felt good to warm my paws, but as soon as I had one warm, the other would freeze again. I had no choice. I had to keep moving.

I trotted down the path to the main road and was immediately met by a tractor-trailer roaring by, spraying snow and ice and slush. I hid behind a tree as it fell in a wave, barely missing me. Peering out, no cars coming, I stepped onto the smooth road where the snow was not nearly as deep because of the vehicles passing over it. I knew it was dangerous to be on the road, but I couldn't walk through a half foot of snow anymore. Cats weren't meant for this kind of travel.

Whenever I saw a car, I'd jump over to the side and hide in the snowbank, shivering in the cold until the car passed. Then, I'd be on my way again. I must have been lost in my thoughts when I suddenly noticed a car was almost directly on top of me, its headlights blinding me. I was about to be run over, and I ran farther into the road to try to avoid the car. I slipped on the snow as my paws went in different directions and barely made it to the other side. I heard the car skip on the icy road as the tires slammed into the snowbank with a loud 'whummph'. Scared, I hopped over the edge of the snow until I heard a man call my name.

"Buck!"

Half-buried at the side of the road, I turned and lifted my snow-covered head. It was Detective Shaw in his cruiser. I'd never been so happy to see him.

CHAPTER 16

Dealership

Shaw took off his fur-lined patrol jacket, made a bed for me on the passenger seat, and directed the heater vents my way. I don't think I'd stopped purring since he'd picked me up in his arms.

"What're you doing way out here, buddy? It's cold! There's a storm coming in, you crazy cat." He kept one hand on me and drove carefully with the other. "You've never gone this far from home." He turned to me. "Don't ever do that again." I closed my eyes slowly and opened them back up. *Yes, sir.*

The heat blew against my fur, lifting it and warming the skin underneath. I bit at my paws, making sure there was no ice stuck within the pads. I licked at the dust and dirt on my fur, which tasted bitter, so I concentrated on my paws and face instead. Burying my cold nose into the soft lining of the jacket, I was finally warming up. Shaw took his cell phone, pressed a few buttons, and lifted it to his ear.

"Guess who I found?"

I could hear Catherine on the other end, happy. I wasn't sure what she was saying, but it was nice to know I was missed.

"I'll keep him with me. Be back soon," Shaw said and hung up.

"We're too far to take you home, bud. I've got a stop to make, and then I'll take you back. You can stay in the car and warm up."

"Central to 84 Adam." The police radio was loud and harsh. Shaw reached under the dash to grab the mic.

"84 Adam, go ahead."

"Will, I've got Mrs. Baer on the line. Third time she's called. Wanted to know an ETA." Penny was the dispatcher, an older woman who always wore a sweater, even on the hottest days. But she was nice.

"Tell her I'm on my way to Dale's place, and then I'll be over. Hopefully, I won't be too long."

"Got it."

"Oh, and tell Tabs her buddy says hello."

My ears perked up.

It was another ten minutes until I saw the tall oval Dale Sharpe Cadillac sign illuminated in the snow. I had my paws up on the window. There were at least six inches on the new cars in the lot, but even in this weather, it looked like a couple of people were shopping for cars. There were two vehicles parked near the entrance. They should have been at the Piggly before it closed, not shopping for a Cadillac. Shaw pulled up next to them and put the cruiser in park.

"Stay here, buddy. Hopefully, I won't be too long." He kept the engine running, grabbed his jacket from under me, and opened the door, stepping out into the falling snow. I put my paws up on the dash, looking through the tinted glass walls of the Cadillac showroom. I was worried about Shaw running into Toli, Dale's bodyguard. That guy seemed like a villain from an 80s action movie.

Speaking of Dale, he ran out the front door, grabbing his red overstuffed winter jacket. He was still putting it on while jogging out to Shaw.

"Officer... Dale Sharpe, King of Cadillacs..." He stuck out his hand. "How can I help you?"

Shaw stopped and looked at the man, taking his hand and giving it a small but firm shake. "Detective William Shaw. How about we go inside and talk about it? Little cold out here."

Dale laughed. "Yeah... umm, okay, but I've got clients, wealthy clients, customers you understand, inside. You hear what I'm saying? I'd rather not have a policeman... don't get me wrong, I love policemen, you know, you guys do a great job and you keep this town safe and all, I get it but... maybe we can talk out here?"

"You don't mind sitting in the back?"

Dale looked at the back passenger door. "You're not gonna lock it on me are you?" He chuckled nervously.

"Naa. Just a few questions is all."

Shaw opened the back door. Dale slipped inside, and the door shut with a solid thunk.

Shaw sat in the front and closed the door, finally out of the cold, and turned to talk to Dale through the black metal grate.

"I see this is a cat-friendly vehicle," Dale said.

"Found him by the side of the road. So, Mr. Sharpe..."

"Dale, please."

"I got a call today from Mrs. Ruth Baer. Her husband works for you. Bernard."

"Ah. Bern. He get in trouble over at the Cherokee Casinos again?"

"He's been missing since Tuesday, Mr. Sharpe. Today is Thursday. Have you not missed him at work? His wife says he's one of your top salesmen."

Dale swallowed. "Well… we only have three. So, I guess he is one of the best."

I turned my head to glance out the front windshield. The pretty woman from the video shoot was looking through the glass from what was, perhaps, her office. Now, she wore a name tag. Val. I turned back.

"You didn't think it was odd he didn't show up yesterday or today?"

"Sometimes our salespeople make their own hours, and maybe today with the storm, you know, he thought traffic was gonna be slow. I mean… we have some people, but, you know, they're not knocking down the doors to buy cars today."

"Does Mr. Baer keep regular hours with you?"

Dale seemed to ponder this question. "Umm, well, you know his wife's been ill with the, the cancer. So… I let him be a little more flexible than my other salesmen."

"I'm sorry to hear that. How long has that been going on?"

"Her thing? Her… illness? I'd say, since the summer, maybe?" Shaw had taken out a short reporter's notepad and was writing in it.

"And when did you last see Mr. Baer?" Shaw continued writing.

"I'd say, it must have been, I guess Monday evening. We locked up together."

"And everything seemed to be okay?"

"Hunky dory. Yup."

"Do you have any idea where he could have gone? His wife is very worried."

"I, ah, I just wouldn't know... he, he is a bit of a card shark. Have you called out to Cherokee?"

I looked around the side of the building where a green dumpster sat against the curb. Five minutes ago, there were no footprints in the snow. Now, there was a set of footprints leading to and from the open dumpster. Odd.

The front door to the dealership opened. Taking up the entire door frame was the thug from the video shoot. Anatoli, in suit and tie. He walked up to Shaw's window and gave it a hard knock, once. Shaw turned and pushed the button to roll down the window. Flakes of snow fluttered inside.

"The phone," he said, "for Mr. Sharpe."

Shaw exhaled. "You're going to have to take a message. He's busy at the moment."

"It is important call."

"And this is a police investigation."

Anatoli looked up into the air and huffed, exhaling a large vapor cloud. He looked back down at Dale, bending at the waist. "Don't bore him with too much talking, yes?"

Shaw rolled up the window, and the large Russian walked back into the dealership. "Friend of yours?"

"He helps."

"Don't have too many Russians here in Copper Summit. What's his name, Mr. Sharpe?"

"Anatoli Zarzandyan. He's Armenian."

"Even less of those. How do you remember that name?"

"We just call him A-to-Z. He does a little bit of everything."

"I see. Like what?" Shaw kept writing.

"Ah, well, he marks up the cars with prices, sells, supervises the mechanics. You know. A bit of everything."

"Seems like a valuable employee."

"Yes."

"How many people work for you?"

"Uh… maybe a dozen?"

"And you own the dealership?"

"Just like the sign says."

"The sign also says you're a king. Just making sure."

Dale cleared his throat. "Officer, I feel like I'm being interrogated here. Did I do something wrong? Should I be concerned?"

"Mr. Sharpe, I'm going to need a list of all your employees with contact numbers and addresses. How long will that take to get to me?"

"This is ridiculous." Dale tried to open the door, but the handle would not engage from the inside. "Unless I'm under arrest, I'd like to go now."

Shaw hesitated. I wasn't sure if he was contemplating taking him in or if he still had more questions to ask. Shaw closed his pad and slipped his pen into a slot at the front of his jacket.

"That's fine, Mr. Sharpe. I'd like you to stay in town for the next few days please, at least until we find Mr. Baer. I'm sure you understand. I'd like that list by the end of the day."

"It is the end of the day."

Sharpe said nothing else as Shaw got out and opened the door for him. He stepped out without a word and walked back to the dealership door. I took the opportunity to slip between Shaw's legs as he yelled, "Buck!"

I hopped through the snow until I reached the dumpster, then leapt up the side onto the open ledge. I sat there until Shaw had no choice but to come after me.

As he approached, he looked at the footprints leading to and away from the dumpster. His eyes narrowed. I'm sure he thought it was completely reasonable for an employee to take out the trash during the very time we were interviewing Sharpe, though it certainly was a convenient time to dump something.

The dumpster smelled horrible, but I jumped inside and went to the lone white bag of trash. I nudged it with my head.

"Good boy," Shaw said, looking over the edge.

"What are you doing…" a deep voice growled from the snow.

CHAPTER 17

Dumpster

It was Anatoli. He approached the opening of the dumpster.

I hopped up to the edge just as Shaw climbed in on the other side.

"Dropped my wedding ring," he said, then picked up the small trash bag. "Ah, here it is."

"No. That is not yours. You put it down," Anatoli commanded, finger pointed. I carefully walked around the inch-wide edge of the dumpster, putting distance between myself and this big man.

"Anatoli? Is that your name?" Shaw started to climb out, putting one foot on the ledge of the sliding door and then hopping over the edge and out, bag in hand.

"Ya."

"I don't know the law in Armenia, but in America, when a person discards trash, they have no reasonable expectation of privacy of those discarded items." He brushed himself off and started to walk toward the cruiser. I hopped along behind him in his footsteps.

"So, for example, if you're thinking that I need a warrant? I don't. Who knows, this could just be scrap paper, right? Or used coffee filters?" He hefted the bag as he walked and took a closer look at the contents through the translucent plastic. "Looks more like documents. Maybe ones that should have been shredded. But there wasn't time to shred them, was there?"

Anatoli took a giant step and moved in front of Shaw, stopping his forward progress.

"We do nothing wrong here. You give me bag." He held his hand out.

"It sounds like you play by Armenian rules. You're out of your league."

Dale appeared through the glass doors, crunching through the snow, this time without his jacket.

"Gentlemen, gentlemen, please… Anatoli, I'll, let me take it from here…"

Anatoli stepped backward, keeping his eyes locked with Shaw's. The snow started to come down heavier. I sat in the last boot print behind Shaw, tail wrapped around my legs, snow gathering on my body.

"Officer, that bag is the property of Dale Sharpe Cadillac, and I'm going to have to ask for it back," said Dale, his voice shaking slightly.

"As I told your friend. It is not yours. Not anymore. Though, if you'd like, either of you can come downtown with me as I empty this bag of trash. Back seat fits three if you'd like to invite another. Four if you get real friendly."

Can cats smile? Yes, they can.

They both looked at each other as Shaw moved around Anatoli, opened the cruiser's front passenger door, and placed the bag on the floor. I jumped in.

"Well, it's an open invitation. And Anatoli, I'll tell you the same thing I told your boss. Stick around. I'm probably going to need you to answer some questions soon."

"He is not my—"

"Ah, Officer," Dale interrupted. "We understand. No traveling. Got it."

Shaw looked at both of them for a moment and then closed the passenger door, walking around to the other side. "I realize it's closing time for you. With this storm coming in, I don't know when we'll talk next. But, Mr. Sharpe, I'd like you to forward that information we talked about before you leave here." He handed Sharpe his card. "Email, fax, however you guys work. I'll have it by six tonight, right?"

Sharpe's jaw was set in place, and his mouth barely moved. "Yes, Officer."

"And if you hear from or see Mr. Baer, you'll call the station immediately."

Anatoli stood like a brick wall behind Sharpe as he answered, "Of course."

We pulled out from the lot, tires crunching through the heavy snow. While Shaw was busy trying to see through the front windshield, I was looking out the back window. Anatoli seemed upset. He pushed Dale toward the entryway, making him stumble. He was speaking to Dale, yelling really, finger raised.

CHAPTER 18

Mrs. Baer

"One more stop, buddy. How'd you know about that bag of trash, huh?" I was curled up on the seat, purring as he scratched under my chin. If Shaw hadn't been turned talking to Dale in the back seat, he would have noticed the tracks too. "Well, thanks, Buck. Might be something here to help us find Mr. Baer, might not. Still, good eyes." I blinked at him. "You make a pretty good detective."

Shaw pulled the mic from under the dash. "84 Adam to Central."

Penny spoke up almost immediately. "84 Adam, go ahead."

"There's something going on down at Dale's place. Not sure what. Heading over to Mrs. Baer now. Should be there in ten. We may need to bring Dale Sharpe in for questioning, but this storm is going to complicate things."

"10-4, Will. If she calls, I'll let her know you're on your way."

The snowflakes were so big it looked like we were flying through feathers. We entered a small neighborhood not far from the center of town, and Shaw pulled up in front of a squat, one-story brick house with smoke coming from the chimney.

"You stay here. I'll be back in a bit." He left the car running, closed the door, and trudged up the sidewalk. I put my paws on the dash and watched him. After a moment, a small older woman opened the front door and waved him in. She had a handkerchief in her hand.

As she stood there, she pointed at the police cruiser. No... she was actually pointing at me. Then, she turned Shaw around, forcing him back out into the snow. He came to the passenger door and scooped me up. "You're in luck," he said, bringing me into the house.

Mrs. Baer immediately stroked me from head to tail as I looked up at her.

"Well, isn't this the cutest little kitty! How dare you, William, leaving him in the car like that on such a day!"

"The heat was on for him, Mrs. Baer."

"Nonsense. A fire is so much better. Isn't that right, good boy?"

"His name is Buck."

"Well, now, Buck, you go on and lay by the fire, and I'll get you a little tuna." She went back to the kitchen as Shaw put me down on the carpet. Shaw stamped his boots on the runner in the hall, then followed me into the living room, occupying one of two deep fabric chairs near the fireplace. I sat next to him and waited.

Mrs. Baer spoke from the kitchen. "I'm worried, William. It's just not like him, and with this snow, I thought maybe he'd been in an accident or... oh dear, I don't know, I hate to even think about it." She returned with a small red pottery bowl with chunk white tuna sticking out from the top and placed it before me. I hadn't eaten in hours and didn't realize how hungry I actually was. I purred and ate in front of the fire while they talked.

She slowly lowered herself into the chair opposite Shaw and dabbed at her eyes. "My first thought was the casinos. It's not like he hasn't done it before. When he gets it into his mind, he can't help himself. But he always drops hints beforehand. Or invites me. But I never go. So loud, those places. Some mornings, I find he's gone, and I assume he's either fishing or up in Cherokee. But that's usually on a weekend, not in the middle of the week. And, like I said, he always lets me know. And today, of course, fishing is out of the question. So… I don't know what to think." She wrung the handkerchief between her fingers.

"The dealership was not much help, unfortunately. They say he keeps odd hours? Because of your… treatments?"

"My treatments?"

"Your cancer…"

She laughed. "Oh, that silly thing. It was a little mole they took off of my ear. A year ago. One procedure. Of course, they look at it every six months, but I don't need any special treatment for that."

Shaw wrote in his notebook. "I see. Well, good. I'm glad it's nothing major."

"I'm fine. I'm just worried about Bernard."

"So Tuesday morning, he went to work, same as usual?"

"Yes, sir, made him coffee, eggs, and toast. Sent him out the door with a ham sandwich in a brown bag. Gave him a kiss, and he was off."

"That was the last you saw him?"

She dabbed at the corner of her eye, and her voice now had a hitch. "Yes."

Shaw reached out and put a hand on her knee. "Ruth, we'll find him. It's a small town. And we'll make some calls up to Cherokee as well. I know some officers up that way. I don't want you to worry."

I finished my tuna, licking my lips and washing my face as Shaw talked, and then I stepped over to Mrs. Baer and brushed against her legs.

"Oh my, what a loving cat," she said, reaching down to pet me. "I used to have my little Sunny, but that was years ago. It's so nice to have a cat in the house. Did you know, Buck, that I was your dad's teacher in the 6th and 7th grades?"

I did not know that.

"Excellent student. So smart you were. And still are."

"Mrs. Baer, was Bernard acting strange lately? Any odd phone calls? Visitors? Anything out of the ordinary?"

"No, nothing. Well… maybe one thing."

"What is it?"

"Tuesday, maybe mid-afternoon? I think he tried to call me. But it didn't go through. My cell phone never rang. I just, all of a sudden, I had a voicemail. But it was just noise. Maybe for a few seconds. And then it cut off."

"But it was from his number?"

"It was. I tried calling back several times, but it just goes to voicemail."

"Mrs. Baer, may I see your phone?"

She got up and went to an end table where her phone was charging. Disconnecting it, she handed it to Shaw.

He scrolled through recent calls and found it.

"4:12, Tuesday afternoon?"

"That sounds right."

"May I play the message?"

"Certainly."

He put it on speaker and hit play. There was static and maybe some talking underneath, but it was very hard to make out because of the overpowering noise. Shaw listened to it several times.

"It's only six seconds long. It seems like it cuts out while someone's speaking."

"Yes. I can't make heads or tails from it."

Shaw listened again. "I think I hear the word 'ate'."

The word was 'late'. I could hear it clearly, but the rest of the words were garbled and shrouded in static.

"Or maybe, 'late'. Do you hear it?" Shaw asked.

"Oh, I can't say I do."

"Does it sound like Bernard?"

"Oh, I don't know about that, possibly, yes."

Shaw thought for a moment. "If it's okay with you, I'd like to take this back to the station, it might help us locate your husband. Do you have a landline for emergencies?"

"Yes, my son insisted that I keep it." She gave him the number, and he wrote it on his pad.

"And who's your carrier?"

"I'm sorry?"

"Your cell phone provider."

"Ah. Atlantic Wireless."

Shaw stood up. "They're about the only choice up here, huh? We just might need to contact them. You've been most helpful, Mrs. Baer, and don't you worry, we'll find Bernard."

"I do hope so. I hated to call the police, I know you're busy, and I didn't want to inconvenience you."

Shaw gently took both of her shoulders in his hands. "You call us for anything you need. Okay?"

"Okay. And thank you for bringing your kitty in. I just couldn't stand knowing he was out in the cold."

"Again, I left the heat on, but I'm sure he's grateful for the tuna."

"Yes, but still, how scared he must have been."

"Not Buck. One more thing, may I take a picture of Bernard?" Shaw lifted a photo of the couple from a table in the foyer. "So I can share it at the precinct."

"Oh. Certainly."

Shaw's cell phone snapped the pic. He put the frame back down and the phone in his jacket pocket. Then, he picked me up, and I settled into his arms, my front paws over his shoulders to look around.

"Thank you, Mrs. Baer. I'll be in touch."

"Please find him, William." She placed a hand on Shaw's arm.

CHAPTER 19

INTERPOL Report

Detective Shaw brought me into the station with him and kept me in his office. I curled up on a leather chair with my tail over my nose and was just about as comfortable as I'd ever been.

He sat at his desk, typing a report into the computer, often referring to the notes on his pad. His office was spartan and clean. Commendations and pictures of friends, family, and co-workers hung on the walls. A picture of Catherine on his desk. Above the door hung a long wooden sign with the words 'To Protect And To Serve' routed into the old dark blue pine. I was told it once hung in the LAPD during the '60s, where his father served. Over the years, it had been knocked, slapped, and touched as a talisman before a cop left the building if they needed a bit of good luck. The bottom edge was smooth, and the paint faded, letting the pine show through.

"Be back, Buck, stay here," he said as he shoved his old office chair back and stepped from behind his desk. He gave the sign a slap and headed out the door.

Tabitha timed it perfectly and slinked in with a few papers in her mouth. She hopped into the chair next to me and laid them on the corner of Shaw's desk.

"Heard you had a little adventure," she said.

"Mm-hmm. Still trying to feel my nose."

"Aww. Poor baby. I should have brought you coffee."

"Looks like you were already carrying a mouthful."

"Indeed. The official INTERPOL records on your new friends, Anatoli Zarzandyan and Lev Luzhkov."

I jumped down from my chair and into hers as she moved just enough to make room for me. We both stared down at the glossy faxed pages, our front paws on the desk. "How did you get these?"

"I could take all the credit for it, but Shaw is probably pulling this same information off the telex as we speak."

I looked them over. These reports were much more substantial than the American ones I had seen on Lev earlier in the motel room. There were a number of pages here, with Tabitha's wet teeth marks at the top corner. I read about Lev first.

Lev Luzhkov. One of the ugliest, most brutal men I had not only the displeasure of seeing but meeting firsthand. He was born into a Balkan crime family stationed in one of Russia's most eastern cities, far from Moscow at the edge of Siberia. There, the family crime syndicate monitored mining operations for the larger organizations closer to Moscow. Lev grew up trading smuggled, uncut diamonds in exchange for personal and business protection in the coastal cities of Sokol, Magadan, and Yamsk. All in the inhospitable but mineral-rich area of the Magadan Oblast. Rugged, mountainous, and unspeakably cold. Lev started as a runner at the age of eight, getting things for his superiors: food, messages, and weapons. Sometimes, small bags of rubies or emeralds were used as a payoff or bribe. Over the years, he proved he could be trusted, until his 17th birthday. He was chosen to broker the peace between the Balkan mob and the Armenian syndicate far to the south.

As a show of good faith, the Armenian representatives would travel almost 12,000 kilometers by train, ferry, and unpaved road to the coastal city of Gorod Magadan. In return, the Armenians would receive a bag of mined jewels valued in the millions. The Russians would also take over a small part of the territory currently held by the Armenians. Everyone agreed, the deal was struck, and the meeting took place. But Lev never showed up with the jewels.

Both groups were furious. The Armenians for having traveled all that way with nothing to show for it, and the Balkans for realizing the man they'd been grooming to lead this faction was, indeed, a traitor.

There was more, but I pushed the Lev section off the desk to get to Anatoli.

"Hey! It took me a while to get those!"

"We don't have a lot of time," I said. "At least, not here. Let me read this before he gets back."

Tabitha jumped down and collected the papers with her paw, tidying them up and pushing them under the chair.

There wasn't as much on Anatoli. He was from the Armenian side, recruited as a young boy after the country declared independence from Russia in the early '90s. He was separated from his family during the Azerbaijani conflict, and there was no mention of them after 1991. Having nowhere else to turn, he became an informant for the Armenian syndicate, using his young age to his advantage. He learned to box. He worked out with the enforcers at the mob-run gym. After several years of watching, learning, and studying the work of those who murdered individuals who didn't cooperate with the syndicate's wishes, he became an enforcer himself.

Most of his time was spent as a bodyguard for the upper echelon. Occasionally, though, he would be asked to put pressure on a certain business owner or politician. Anatoli enjoyed those moments. Then, there were times when he would be asked to take a life. These moments weren't as pleasurable for him, mostly because he was responsible for clean-up as well.

INTERPOL was able to backtrack Anatoli's entry into the States, discovering that he arrived at JFK International under the name Alexi Grigoryan in 2016. He had not been seen since.

Shaw's footsteps approached his office. I pushed the rest of the papers down to Tabitha, who hurriedly slid them under the leather chair, hiding them from view. Then she jumped gracefully into the second chair, turned a few times, and put her head on her front paws. Shaw walked in.

"Ah... I see you two are catching up. You'd be proud of Buck, Tabs. He's been a very brave kitty. Haven't you, Buck?"

I do not like being called a kitty. Though it did make Tabitha smile a bit. So I guess it was alright.

Shaw sat down, slapped a folder on his desk, and gently set his coffee mug down as some pages rustled. Tabitha turned her head to me and then nodded toward the break room. I shook my head no.

After a few minutes, my patience paid off. Jay knocked on Shaw's door frame.

"Gotta see this, Will." He walked in, laid a few pages onto Shaw's desk, and stepped back. "One, thanks for the bag of trash you left me to sift through. Had to open my window in 20-degree weather. Two, take a look at what's in the folder. Either the King of Cadillacs doesn't own a shredder, or they're taking loan applications and committing some kind of identity fraud. Those SS numbers, bank accounts, all that stuff should be destroyed immediately. Not thrown into a dumpster a few months later."

Shaw paged through the applications in the folder. "Not a crime to have a folder of loan applications."

"Not a crime, no. But... unusual. To say the least. And look at the dates on those things. Some of them are over a year old."

"Yeah. Does seem odd..."

"Also, the last page there. From Global Shipping, out of the Port of Wilmington." Shaw pulled out the page and looked at it. "Outbound container 8873FHH. What does it say is in it?"

Shaw traced his finger down the paper. "Umm, ten king-sized mattresses."

"How big is a king, Will?"

He put the page down and typed on his keyboard. After a moment, he said, "80x76. Depth varies."

"And how big is a shipping container?"

More typing. "Ahh, 40 feet by 8 feet by 9 feet. Approximate. I think I see where you're going with this..."

"Don't bother with the math. I've already done it. You could fit three to four cars into a container, plus leave room for ten mattresses to put in front of them by the cargo doors."

"So they're shipping vehicles out of the States to... where?"

"There's no information on that, at least on what we could recover."

Shaw's phone buzzed, and he picked it up.

"Yup," he said, still looking at the shipping container bill. "You're kidding. When?" Shaw looked up at Alvarez, still in the doorway. He hung up the phone.

"Bernard Baer's home."

CHAPTER 20

Courtland County Map

"I need to get back to the office," I told Tabitha. Shaw had left to talk to Alvarez at his desk. She collected the INTERPOL faxes from under the chair with her paw, then held them between her teeth to neatly deposit them in Shaw's waste bin.

"Hopefully, he won't see those," she said.

We walked together down the hallway, side by side. Mary, the desk officer, saw us from her station and said, "Well, bless their hearts."

It wasn't like our tails were entwined together. I sometimes just don't understand humans.

"What about Mr. Baer?" Tabitha asked.

I whispered to her. "I'm sure Shaw is on the phone with them right now, asking if he can come over. He's not one to do much work over the phone. But…" I looked around to see if anyone was nearby. "I want to take a good look at that map just inside the station doors."

"What for?"

"I need to see if I can figure out where that waterfall is. I had no idea we had one in Courtland County."

"Dummy, they don't mark waterfalls on maps."

I peered around the corner toward the front sliding glass doors. "It's clear. Keep an eye out for me."

"For what?"

Two old, high-backed chairs were set against the wall near the doors. A long, thin table sat between them, with an old phone and some brochures about crime prevention and safety. A map of Courtland County hung behind glass on the wall above the table.

"I don't know. People."

I hopped up on the chair, then the table, and stood on my hind legs to peer up at the map.

It was a topographical map with elevation lines. I stretched out to reach near the middle and traced my paw from about where our house was, down 163 for a few miles, but couldn't see the turnoff on the left that Lev Luzhkov had taken. I sighed.

But wait… with elevations…

I looked back up. Again, I took my paw, but this time found the river. It ran somewhat parallel to 163, but then started to veer away from it, north. I knew somewhere along the flow of the river, there was a drop-off. A steep one. At least a hundred feet.

"What are you doing?" Tabitha whispered.

"Looking for isohypses…"

"Iso what?"

"Shhhh. Contour lines."

My paw kept moving along the blue line of the river until it hit several contours close together. I searched for the small numbers. There they were. Elevation at the bottom was 3246. Top elevation was 3420. I found my waterfall.

"Got it. It looks like it's about… a hundred and forty-some feet."

"How come I've never heard of it?"

I looked a little more carefully at the map. The part of the map where the waterfall stood was in a darker green area, crooked and oblong, outlined in dots. In the middle of the area were the words: COURTLAND COUNTY STRICT NATURE RESERVE.

"It's protected. There must be fencing around it or something." I jumped down.

"So the tunnels, they go under it?"

"Looks like it. Yes."

"Do they… murder people and get rid of bodies there?" Tabitha swallowed.

"I think that's what we need to find out."

"You. That's what you need to find out."

"Yeah. That's what I meant."

I heard Shaw and Alvarez coming down the main hall. They were talking about Mr. Baer. I looked over to Tabitha.

"I'm not buying it," Shaw said.

"Agreed. He's hiding something," Alvarez answered as they rounded the corner.

"Alright. I'm headed back over there. I can tell you this, though, Ruth knows nothing about what happened. I know you're relatively new to town…"

"I moved here 15 years ago, man."

"That's a newcomer up here. Anyway, Mrs. Baer was my 5th grade teacher. She probably still thinks I'm ten years old. But I've known her for a long time, and she's as in the dark as we are."

Alvarez nodded outside to the growing storm. The snow looked purple as the skies darkened, and it was so heavy I couldn't even see across the street. "How about you take the Tahoe? I'll stay here with Mary. I'm thinking it might be better to hang here than go home."

"Na. I'll take the cruiser back to the house and get my Suburban. Thanks though. You sure you're good here?" He bent down to pick me up, then stroked underneath my chin. I closed my eyes and smiled.

"Yup. Miss Mary and I can play cards if we get bored. And when you're done over there, give me a call. I'd love to hear his story."

Shaw nodded and walked through the first glass door as it slid open to the foyer. The cold hit me immediately. "If you get really bored, I have a few Michael Connelly novels on my bookshelf," said Shaw, looking over his shoulder.

"Thanks. I don't read."

"And it shows."

I waved goodbye to Tabitha. She blinked back.

Shaw zipped me up inside his jacket. He'd kept the cruiser running, so it was warm inside. I poked my head out as he unzipped a bit and pulled out into the storm.

So Bernard Baer wasn't the dead man I'd seen being dragged through the tunnel. But something told me that Mr. Baer knew who that man was. In fact, Mr. Baer probably knew a whole lot about what was going on at the dealership.

I took one last look out at the snowstorm as Shaw drove home to get the Suburban. It was about a 10-minute drive on a normal day — double that with this snow. I settled into a warm ball, still zipped up comfortably in his jacket. I hoped that he'd take me with him to the Baer's. Something told me that whatever he found out there could crack this case wide open.

CHAPTER 21

Catnap

"Buck!" yelled Patrick, rushing up to his dad and stroking my head as I peeked out from his jacket.

Catherine had lit a fire, making the living room warm and toasty. She walked to her husband and gave him a hug, squeezing me between them. I meowed and jumped down. I avoid being squashed as much as possible.

"I was worried. The weather service said it's getting worse, and I hadn't heard from you…"

"Sorry, hun. Should have called you from the station. But I have to go back out." He hugged her closer now that I was gone.

"What? Why?"

"Ruth Baer may need my help." I ran over to the fireplace, Patrick chasing me. Flopping to my side, I welcomed his warm hands running over my fur.

"Well, I kind of need you here too…"

"Do you?" Shaw said with a smile.

Catherine grabbed her husband's hands and lowered her voice. "Yes. It's not funny. I'm worried about Lev what's his name, and I spend my time looking out the front window making sure he doesn't sneak up."

"Catherine, he's long gone by now. Besides, I'd never leave you guys alone if I thought he was nearby. Please, don't worry."

"That's not how I work."

Shaw made some coffee to fill a tall thermal mug while he talked with the kids about making a snowman tomorrow. There had only been one large snow so far this winter, and this one was somewhat unexpected. The kids were excited. Well, Patrick more than Frannie, though she did like a good snowball fight.

"I'll be back soon." Shaw kissed his wife and headed for the door. I jumped up, nudged against Patrick, and ran to the door as well.

"Oh, no, you don't. You've had enough adventure for one day," he said, looking down at me. I stood up and put my front paws against the door and meowed.

"He said no, Buck, now come on…" Catherine tried to shoo me away as Shaw opened the door, but I slipped through and made it outside. I stood on the front porch, looking back.

"Buckleberry, get in here this instant!" Catherine yelled at me from the doorway, her voice disappearing into the snow.

Shaw laughed. "It's okay. I'll take him for a ride. It would make Ruth happy to see him again."

He scooped me up and held me under his arm, carrying his thermal mug in the other hand. He turned back to his wife.

"Listen, I'm going to leave the patrol car running, lights on. Will that make you feel better?"

She pouted. "Fine. Just get back here soon."

"I promise." Another peck at the door, and we were off.

The Suburban was cold. Shaw dumped me onto the front seat and went to start the cruiser. He put the headlights on, and the beams cut through the heavy snow. Then he closed the door and came back to the truck.

"You ready, Buck?" He took off his glove and scratched my head. I meowed in return.

He'd brought his hand-held radio with him and called into the station.

"84 to Base."

A brief pause, and Mary radioed back. "Go ahead 84."

"Headed over to Ruth's now. What's the weather, Mary? Am I gonna get stuck in this thing?"

"Right now they're calling for 2 feet by morning, Will. Glad you decided to change vehicles. I'll let Jay know what you're up to."

"Thanks. I'll call him when I'm done."

When the engine had warmed, Shaw adjusted one of the blower vents to hit me just right. There's nothing like a blast of hot air on a cold winter night. I curled up on the seat and closed my eyes.

My stomach rumbled. I didn't even think to eat at the house with Shaw leaving again so quickly. But it seemed like Shaw intended to bring me into the Baer's house again. I'd happily eat the other half of that can of tuna.

Truthfully, I could use some quiet time to try to sort things out. Every piece of this puzzle was like a string dangling in front of me, and if I hit one with my paw, it hit another until soon, all the strings were moving in different directions. Between my hunger and my need to go over everything I'd learned in the last few days, I was doubting my decision to take this ride with Shaw. A bowl of my food and some nipped Earl Grey in my quiet office now seemed like a better use of my time.

I opened my eyes and uncurled myself, standing up and putting my front paws on the dash. I looked out at the drifting snow and then over to Shaw. I meowed, hoping he'd get the message and turn the Suburban around for me.

"Yeah, buddy, I know. It's really coming down."

Humans. Why don't they understand?

I stepped back to the seat, turned a few times, and put myself back into a ball. Within a few minutes, I was fast asleep.

My catnap produced a dream — half productive, half terrifying. It started with the Coupe DeVille, driving slowly past Room 12 of the Highlander Motel, only this time, I was sitting outside, watching the car from underneath the overhang of the roof. Yellow headlights cut through the falling snow. But as it started to move past me, it stopped. The passenger door creaked open. Lev's huge black shadow motioned me in, the end of his cigarette bright orange. For some reason, I obeyed. I scurried underneath the front seat, pushing a knife aside.

"Where are we going?" I asked from my hiding spot.

"To see my son," he said. Now, Lev could speak English. And understand cats, apparently. He took a sip of beer from the can in his hand.

Somehow, when the car stopped in the middle of the woods, I escaped. I made it to the tunnels, but as I ran through the darkness, I felt myself being picked up. I tried to fight, but it was no use. Whoever it was that caught me wrapped me up in a black peacoat. Toli's coat. Suddenly, I was back in the Cadillac and thrown into the rear seat. Anatoli threw his jacket in the back with me. I hid in the back window, as far away as I could possibly get.

"Where are we going?" I asked again.

"The docks," was his answer.

Soon, we arrived, parking directly in front of a red shipping container, the headlights illuminating the padlock on the steel handle.

Anatoli got out, slammed the door shut before I could escape, and opened the container. The wide doors creaked just like the door of the DeVille. He went around the back, pushed the car into the empty container, and slammed the doors shut with a loud clang. But the car didn't stop, it kept moving forward, tilting as it moved, gathering speed, its momentum now unstoppable as it tilted more and more until it was falling, surrounded by torrents of water, dropping like a stone as the icy green water fell all around the car, and that's when I startled awake and was suddenly on all fours in Shaw's front seat.

"You okay, Buck?"

I shook my head. I was okay. And now I knew two things — there were two pieces of evidence to examine. One was at the bottom of the waterfall; the second was the beer can Lev had left somewhere in Shaw's shed.

CHAPTER 22

Mr. Baer

Animals have a much harder time lying than humans do. At least, that's what I've come to learn. So, approaching a human with a healthy mistrust is always my first course of action. When, or if, they prove themselves trustworthy, then I can start to break down some of the natural barriers I've put into place. This is the cat's way.

Bernard Baer seemed nice enough, though nervous to see Shaw on his front doorstep. But there was something about him that I didn't trust. He was nothing like his wife, who reached out for me from the front door as I fell against her without fighting. She took me in from the cold and sat with me in the chair by the fire. She repeatedly told Shaw how glad she was that her husband was back without incident, thanking him for his help and apologizing for overreacting.

"It was not an overreaction, Mrs. Baer. Your husband, for a time, was truly missing."

Bernard scoffed. "I told you, Will, it was just a breakdown."

His story was suspect at best. From what Mr. Baer had told Shaw, who wrote everything in his pad, the following happened: A shipment of cars was due in Wilmington, but the driver of the car hauler called out sick. Baer was the only other employee with a CDL, a Commercial Driver's License, from being a long-distance truck driver years back. He was asked to drive down to the port, a 5-hour trip one way, to pick up vehicles. The engine overheated. He tried calling, but his cell service didn't work outside the mountains.

"I'm telling you, Will, the rig just broke down! That's it, nothing else. If I didn't have such a piece of junk for a phone, my calls would have gone through."

Mrs. Baer kept busy petting me, not defending her husband, not coming to his rescue. I was sure it was because she knew her husband was lying, or at least that some things weren't making sense. I'm certain that Shaw thought the same thing.

"Take me through it again, Bernard."

"But I just told you!"

Shaw was taking notes. He didn't look up as he spoke again. "From the beginning."

Mr. Baer huffed from his side of the couch. Shaw was sitting opposite him on the other side. He looked up.

"Bernard. I have to tell you that nothing's adding up here. You say you were told to drive the trailer down to Wilmington to pick up a shipment of cars. Fine. But you didn't tell your wife before you left? Then didn't call her the whole time you were gone?"

Mr. Baer was sweating, and he wiped his upper lip with the sleeve of his flannel shirt. "Look, I know. I know I was dumb. It's just, I didn't have my medicine, and I thought it would just take a few hours to fix the stupid trailer…"

"I assume you slept at a hotel for a few nights?"

"Of course."

"Which one?"

"I… I don't think I remember that, maybe a Motel 6? There's so many."

"But your credit card statement should let us know where you stayed. Right?" Shaw kept his eyes on Bernard.

"Oh. I, ah, used cash."

"Bernard!" exclaimed Mrs. Baer. "We don't have hundreds of dollars lying around! How much did it cost? Why didn't you use the card?"

"I don't know! I had the cash! It was easier that way!" he yelled back at his wife. I put my ears back and looked up at her. She seemed shocked and put her hand to her mouth. "Ruth, I'm sorry… I'm just tired, and after all this, I need to rest for a bit."

She got up from her chair, holding me, and walked to the kitchen without saying a word. She put me down and went to the fridge. She wiped away a tear from her eye.

"How about you finish that tuna from this morning?"

I purred and rubbed against her legs. She took a small ceramic bowl from the fridge and placed it on the floor. I ate from it as she filled another bowl with water from the sink.

Shaw was talking in the living room. "I want to believe you. I really do. The last thing I want to do is bring you down to the station, but Bernard, this just isn't making sense. Are you in some kind of trouble there at the dealership?"

"What? No. That's ridiculous."

Shaw said nothing.

I finished the tuna, lapped at some water, and then walked back to the living room. I settled down in front of the fire.

"Bernard. Please. Give me something here."

He said nothing for a moment, then looked up at Shaw, eyes wet. His hands were clasped together, trembling. "Will, I never meant to…"

A sudden, sharp crack filled the room, and glass shattered everywhere. The lamp next to Mr. Baer exploded into a thousand pieces, and he fell back onto the couch. There were more shots. Instinctively, I ran underneath the armchair where Mrs. Baer had held me, eyes as wide as they could get. Shaw jumped to his feet, hand on the butt of his service revolver. He fell to the floor and crawled to the smashed front window. Snow streamed in, and the room was instantly cold. He peeked over the ledge.

Mrs. Baer screamed and stepped into the living room.

"Ruth! Down!" said Shaw, motioning her back.

"Oh my goodness! Bernard!" She ran to him on the couch. He started to sit up, but Shaw told them again to stay down. Then, in one quick motion, he was on his feet and rushing to the front door. "Get to the back of the house, both of you. Call 911." And then he was out the door.

I climbed out from under the chair and hopped onto the built-in cushions at the front window, trying to avoid the giant shards of glass. The wind and snow flew into the room. I heard Shaw calling for backup on his radio as he hid behind the Suburban. I jumped out of the broken window.

The cold seeped into my paws as I crouched in the deep snow. It was already above my head, and I had to stand up a bit on my hind legs to see out of the hole I had created. A dark SUV gunned its engine and fishtailed its way down the street. I lost it in the white swirl of the storm.

Another vehicle snapped its lights on and quickly followed, but I couldn't make out the details. The snow was just too thick.

I hopped out of my hole, and in several short jumps, I was next to Shaw. He scooped me up.

"Ruth!" Shaw called out as he opened the Suburban's door and dumped me onto the seat. She appeared at the window. "Is Bernard alright?"

"Yes, I think so!"

"Help is on the way. You both go into the basement!" Shaw yelled over the wind.

"Oh, dear," said Mrs. Baer, moving away from the window.

Shaw climbed into the front seat and closed the door. "Buddy, you have had an interesting day."

He slammed the Suburban into reverse and quickly backed out of the Baer's driveway. I was thrown forward and steadied myself before I slid off the seat.

"You'd do better down there," he said, nodding to the footwell under the dash. He floored the accelerator, the fat tires gripping the snow, and pushed me back against the seat. "Buck, get down there." He tried to push me down, but I didn't let him. Finally, he ignored me and concentrated on driving, making sure his seatbelt was secure.

"You're a stubborn cat."

He was right. I wasn't going to miss this.

There was no way anyone was out driving in this storm, let alone two vehicles back to back. I wasn't sure if we'd be able to catch up to the SUV, but I was almost positive the other vehicle was a sedan. They could only go so fast in this weather, and we had the benefit of being in a vehicle built for snow. I put my paws up on the dashboard and looked out, heart pounding.

There, in the distance, were a pair of tail lights. And we were quickly closing the gap.

CHAPTER 23

Collision

The Suburban was speeding through the snow, engine growling. The wind blew so strong sometimes that it pushed us sideways, and Shaw had to correct it as we slid back into tracks left from the car ahead.

"Buck, come here." Shaw patted his chest. I could tell by the sternness of his voice that he was serious. I climbed into his lap.

While traveling at a completely unsafe speed through the snowstorm, he pulled me to him, pushing me inside his fur-lined jacket and zipping it up a bit. I settled in against him.

"Hold on."

Peeking out of the top, eyes wide, we gained on the car in front of us. It looked like a silver sedan, and it was moving way too fast, the back tires slipping and sliding. I wasn't sure what Shaw was going to do, but it didn't involve braking. In fact, he pushed the accelerator to the floor, closed the gap, and slammed into the back right corner of the car. It jolted me forward against Shaw's jacket, and I heard a loud crunch.

The sedan spun out of control, headlights making the snow glitter in a circle like a lighthouse searchlight. Shaw tapped the brakes and kept some distance between us and the spinning car. Its tires could no longer grip, and the car went into another revolution, bouncing against a guard rail with a loud clang and sliding to the other side of the road. The front of the silver car crashed into the snowbank, crumpling the front end. It finally came to a halt, the front end tilted into the snow. The back tires were up in the air, still spinning.

Shaw slowed and pulled the Suburban to a stop perpendicular to the road. We couldn't see the driver on the other side of the car.

He unzipped his jacket. I jumped out onto the seat as he opened his door and stepped out, withdrawing his revolver with his right hand and switching his MagLite on with his left, stacking his hands on top of each other. He stood behind the engine block and wheel and pointed the weapon and beam at the dented sedan. He spoke loudly over the wind. "This is Copper Summit Police! You are under arrest! Exit the vehicle with your hands up!"

Nothing happened for a few moments. Shaw repeated himself. Then, I heard a loud creak as the dented door opened from the driver's side.

"Hands up!" Shaw yelled.

After a few seconds, a pair of gloved hands appeared from behind the car, reaching into the air. One of the hands held something dark and square.

"Drop whatever it is you're holding! Now!"

A head appeared. One I recognized. It was the woman from the video shoot and the dealership. Her long blonde hair blew sideways in the wind, obscuring part of her face, but I was sure it was her. And whatever it was she held, she did not let go. Her golden hair gleamed in the bright beam of Shaw's Maglite.

"I said drop it!"

The woman fell to the ground silently, disappearing behind the silver car.

"Get off the ground and stand up!"

There was no response. Shaw repeated his command.

Nothing. The wind blew the snow so hard that it was difficult to see even five feet in front of us.

"Dammit..." Shaw said under his breath. Stepping out from the safety of the Suburban's hood, he slowly approached the car. The bright beam lit up the snow before him. I jumped down and followed.

Shaw carefully approached the vehicle, but he couldn't see what I could. From my low vantage point, I saw the woman on the ground, arms out to her sides. Blood spilled from her head.

Shaw rounded the back end of the sedan and aimed the circle of light at the woman. She was dressed in dark slacks, gloves, and a white winter jacket.

"Do not move," he told her. Shaw made sure her hands were empty and then stepped up to her, leaving about a foot of space between them.

"On your feet. Now."

She didn't respond. The wound from her forehead bled into the snow.

Carefully, he stepped closer, revolver still at the ready, and pointed in her direction. She wasn't moving. He shone the light on a square black wallet on the ground, which held her badge and credentials:

**FEDERAL BUREAU OF INVESTIGATION •
DEPARTMENT OF JUSTICE
SPECIAL AGENT VALERIE HAYES**

CHAPTER 24

Valerie

Shaw had carefully laid her in the back seat of the Suburban, and with the First Aid kit in the back, he cleaned the wound to her head the best he could, but it still bled. He propped her head up with his jacket rolled into a ball and covered her with a blanket retrieved from the back. She still hadn't moved. He got back into the front seat and reached for his handheld.

"Central, come in."

It took a few moments. Penny must have been coordinating more than a couple of things back at the station, but she came on after a few seconds.

"Will, are you okay?"

"I'm okay. If you haven't already, I need you to get Emergency Services out to the Baer's place and put out a BOLO on a dark SUV coming from that location. No plate number. Probably speeding. Get Jay out there now. All available officers need to patrol from town outwards, say 20 miles."

"EMS is already on their way. Ruth said he wasn't hurt, just scared."

"He'll need to be checked over. Listen. I've got a bit of an issue here. Got into an incident with an FBI agent, and she's hurt. I'm going to try to make it to the hospital, but if conditions get worse, I'm closer to home and may end up there."

"Did you say FBI?"

"Affirmative. She has a head injury from a vehicle collision. I'll let you know where I end up. But get Jay looking out there now."

"Dark SUV. Got it."

"Over and out."

He slowly moved the Suburban forward, straightening it out, and with the edge of the front bumper, he pushed the back end of the sedan until it slid parallel with the road. It wasn't completely off the road, but hopefully it would be seen if someone was crazy enough to be driving in this weather. If he had the cruiser, he'd have put strobes or cones out.

I looked over my seat into the back. Val was lying there, covered in a blanket, Shaw's jacket under her head. She moved with the motion of the Suburban as we traveled as fast as we could to the hospital.

I carefully stepped up to the top edge of the seat, then jumped down next to her, curling up at her stomach.

"84 to Central."

"Here Will."

"Just a head's up I'm taking her back to my place. Roads are bad, but the blowing snow is making it a whiteout. Home's not far."

"10-4. Be careful. Jay's out there, and at least one other."

"Do me a favor and call my neighbor Whitney Porter. If she's not stuck at the hospital. She's a nurse. And call Cathy, let her know what's going on."

"Will do, no worries. You keep your eyes on the road."

The car swayed as the wind hit it. It was mid-afternoon, but it looked like dusk.

"You two alright back there?" Shaw asked, briefly looking over his shoulder. Well, I was alright. Hopefully, Val would be okay as well.

Mrs. Porter lived next door to us and was a not-quite-elderly nurse at Courtland General. Sometimes I'd see her in the early morning coming home from an overnight shift. She'd always say hi as I jaunted through her yard on the way back to the office from wherever I'd been. She'd know how to help.

It took maybe another 10 minutes to get to our house. Catherine ran out with a coat wrapped around her as soon as she saw the headlights pull in.

"My God, Will, what happened?"

He had just come through the door with Val in his arms. He laid her gently on the couch.

"Is Whitney here yet?"

"Not yet. Mary said you were in an accident? Who's this?"

"She's FBI. I didn't know. I pushed her off the road with the SUV, thought she was someone else." Catherine held her hand up to her mouth.

There was a knock at the door. I stood up and went to the door along with Shaw. The cold hit hard as soon as he opened it to let Whitney Porter in. She snuck in fast and shut the door behind her.

"Whew. This is as bad as '96."

"Thank you for coming, Whit. Sorry to call you out in this."

"Bah," she said with a wave of her hand. "I was supposed to be at General two hours ago, but they told me to stay home. Whoever's there now is stuck for a bit. Who do we have here?" She approached the couch and gently sat on the corner. Catherine had already taken Val's white jacket off.

Will sighed. "This is Valerie Hayes, she's an FBI agent. And I ran her off the road before I knew that."

"I see," said Whitney. "Seems like you got some 'splainin' to do," she said, looking at Will. With a slight groan, she knelt slowly on her knees next to Val's head.

"So she hit her head looks like…" Whitney pulled some of Val's bloody blonde hair away to examine the wound. "Steering wheel?" She looked up at Shaw.

"Well, that would mean she wasn't wearing her seatbelt."

"Then, she wasn't wearing her seatbelt," she said, matter-of-factly.

Whitney checked Val's vitals, feeling her arms and legs and lifting her eyelids.

"Just strange. In the storm and all."

"Fine. You think about that while I look her over. We might not know much until she wakes up, though."

"You think she will?"

She chuckled a bit. "Wake up? Yeah. Soon, I think. No bleeding from the ears, pulse okay, some bruising, but that might be the worst of it. Now, when she does wake up, that might be a different story."

Confident Valerie was going to recover, Will put on a pot of coffee as Whitney and Catherine went to the kitchen nook to sit down and talk.

Now was the perfect time to head back to the office. I could keep an eye on the ladies through the window, and if they left the table, I'd come back in. It felt like it'd been days since I sat at my desk, and in fact, I'd honestly lost track of time. I slipped through the cat door and bounded through the snow, hop by hop.

CHAPTER 25

Office Hours

I was happy to finally be back at the office, but I needed to dig my way to the door before I could enter. There was a massive mound of snow blocking me from even seeing it.

I set upon using my paws to dig out the powdery fluff when suddenly I hit something hard, almost like a rock. Well, no wonder the snow was so high here, I thought, someone had placed a rock in front of my door. But what sense did that make? My paws continued to dig. And strangely, I began to see a pattern on the rock. One that looked suspiciously like a turtle's shell.

Mr. Tuttle began to move, slowly at first, and then he walked away, snow falling from him as the powdery mound collapsed. He poked his head out from his snow-covered shell and turned toward me.

"Mr. Buckleberry. It is me once more, Mr. Tuttle." He extended an icy appendage toward me. It was more like a webbed foot-like flipper thing and entirely inappropriate for shaking. So, I touched it instead.

"Yes, I remember. You… seemed to be upset the last time we met."

"And wouldn't you be if someone stole your house?"

"I suppose I would, Mr. Tuttle, yes. Well, it's rather cold out here, how about we talk inside?"

"You think you're cold? I've been waiting outside for..." I let the turtle talk as I unlocked the wooden door and creaked it open. I held the door for Mr. Tuttle as he slowly moved across the threshold, dragging snow in behind him. Making a mess.

"...can barely feel my feet. Don't you cat detectives have normal business hours?"

Looking up through the side window, I could see Catherine and Whitney Porter at the table, lights low, waiting for Agent Hayes to wake up. I was sure that Shaw was in the living room keeping an eye on her.

"...just absurd that a turtle would have to walk all this way in the middle of a snowstorm..."

I lit some wax-coated Lickers® boxes in the fireplace and put some small kindling on them. I could already feel the heat and put my front paws up to warm them.

"Do you know how long it took me to get here, only to find your office locked and dark?"

As the flames grew, I added some larger logs until the fire had a nice roar.

"...but no, as long as you get your daily rate, I guess it doesn't matter what happens to an insignificant turtle."

I mopped the melting snow from the wooden floor and threw the used towel into the corner. Then, I headed into the kitchen to put on a pot of water.

"...guess Miss Wellington was wrong about you, but you're the only detective in town so I had little choice."

"Tea, Mr. Tuttle?" I asked from the kitchen.

"Oh, yes please, might you have a lavender chamomile?"

I looked through the top cabinet where I kept my myriad of tea selections.

"I'm afraid not," I answered. Honestly, I hated lavender.

"Then anything herbal, I suppose. Though chamomile should be a staple of any good tea hutch."

The water took several minutes to boil, during which time I happily ignored Mr. Tuttle's complaints and held my paws over the open flame.

"...where would one even *put* a turtle's house once they've stolen it? And a house is a heavy thing, you know, especially with all my antiques."

I poured our cups full. "Honey, Mr. Tuttle?"

"Oh. Yes. Thank you. And I don't think I haven't looked up and down the riverbank for it because I have. Twice."

I brought the steaming cups into my office, placing Mr. Tuttle's Tension Tamer in front of him, where he sat on my braided rug. Then I thought for a moment and sat.

"The riverbank?" I asked him.

"Yes, where I live! Honestly, have you not been listening to me?"

I put my Earl Grey on the corner of my desk and walked slowly around to my chair. I sat again, curling my tail around me, and lifted the cup. Blowing. Sipping. Thinking.

"...just gone. One minute, I'm out in the forest looking for twigs, and the next, poof!" He held his appendages up in the air. "Vanished."

"Mr. Tuttle, may I ask you a question?"

"So you're on the clock then. I suppose. Let's just try to keep expenses to a minimum."

"Do you happen to live near a waterfall?"

"Oh, Mr. Buckleberry, you should see the view from my kitchen window. It's the most beautiful thing in the morning because the sun lights it up just perfectly, and it looks like molten gold flowing down the side of the cliff."

"So you're in the Strict Nature Preserve."

"Yes. It's beautiful there. No people, no cars, no noise. Just the sound of the falls. Oh, and the occasional house thief. If I ever catch him…"

"Mr. Tuttle, the area around your house. Well, where it was. Can you describe it?"

"Yes. I built my house among the exposed roots of a Balsam Pine. They line the river there. It added some strength and allowed me to build right on the water."

"Were the roots damaged when you noticed your house was gone? The land around it?"

"I should say so! It was as if someone took a baseball bat to the whole root system and the shoal around it. How rude of them. Like it wasn't enough to steal a turtle's home!"

I nodded. "I agree. Totally uncalled for."

Could Mr. Tuttle's house have been dislodged by another body thrown over the edge of the waterfall? One, perhaps, that was dragging any manner of car parts behind it, digging up the dirt and damaging the roots to Mr. Tuttle's house before washing it away? Mr. Tuttle's first visit to me was before my experience in the tunnel. So it couldn't have been the body that I had seen being dragged.

The storm raged outside, the wind howling through the fireplace.

"When did your house disappear, Mr. Tuttle?"

"The day before the last day of the weekend, Sunday. So… Saturday."

"And today is… Friday."

"Yes? So?"

I was thinking that if there had been another murder, none had been reported. And more than likely, that murder would have occurred one week ago or perhaps a few days earlier. Yet, no report. And if the body had floated downstream, where would it eventually end up? I needed to take another look at a Courtland County map.

But I also needed to look in the shed for the beer can that Lev had left behind. If I could somehow show Shaw and he could run prints, it would prove that Lev had been staking out the house, and perhaps it would lead to his arrest and the family's safety. And I also needed to ID the body at the bottom of the waterfall. It was going to be a busy day.

I looked out the window to make sure Catherine and Mrs. Porter hadn't moved. They hadn't.

"Mr. Tuttle, would you happen to have any friends—"

"Of course I do, I…"

I held up my paw. "Mr. Tuttle. Friends that are… beavers."

He thought for a moment.

"Well, I wouldn't consider him a friend, more of a casual acquaintance. He used to do some plumbing work for me. When I had a house."

"His name?"

"Wait one minute," Mr. Tuttle said, retracting all four appendages, along with his head, into his shell. There were some rustling noises, and after a few moments, his head and feet appeared again. He held something wet and dripping.

"His card," he said and handed it to me. I put on my glasses to read it, letting the card drip onto the floor.

"Ahh. Hamilton Waters, Owner and Proprietor of Busy Beaver Plumbing. Hmm. Original."

"Excuse me, but what does this have to do with me? I'd appreciate it if you attended to your personal home repair issues on your own time—"

"This concerns your case, sir. Would you do me a favor?" I asked, not knowing what kind of response I would get.

"I suppose…"

I opened my drawer and handed Mr. Tuttle my card. "It's laminated," I said. Name, job title, office number, email. Plus, a little silhouette of a black cat. "Please give this to Mr. Waters and have him get in touch with me. Email is best since I'm thinking I'll be out of the office for a bit."

"Okay," said Mr. Tuttle, putting the laminated card into his shell. "But I'm not paying for your plumbing problems."

"Of course not. Now, Mr. Tuttle, where are you staying tonight? You can't be out in this storm without shelter."

"My intention is to walk back to the river and start rebuilding my house."

"Why don't you stay here tonight, and once the weather clears up, you can start on your house?" My tail whacked against the chair. I think a part of me really didn't want him spending the night here, but I couldn't just kick him out in this weather.

He sat there, contemplating. He looked at the roaring fire, then his steaming mug of tea. Looked down at the warm rug. "Alright."

I was expecting him to put up a fight, which I would have immediately conceded to and let him be on his way. Luck wasn't on my side tonight.

Looking up at the Shaw's kitchen window, both ladies were getting up from their chairs. Maybe this was it. Hurriedly, I put my mug in the sink, patted the floor dry where Hamilton Waters' card dripped and then went to the door. I held it open and looked back at Mr. Tuttle.

"If you have to… you know, do your business. Please. Go outside."

Mr. Tuttle's mouth hung open as his little pinhead eyes looked at me. "Do you take me for a barbarian, sir? A lowbrow philistine? I'll have you know—"

I closed the door gently behind me.

CHAPTER 26

Answers

I slipped in through the cat door and walked through the living room to Agent Val Hayes. She was lying on the couch and held an ice pack to her head.

"I, I can't really open my eyes," she said. Whitney had cleaned the wound well. Val winced as she held the ice to her temple.

"It's okay, honey, you just keep your eyes closed for a bit," said Whitney, nodding her head toward the light above. Shaw took the hint, turning off the lights in the living room until only the fire illuminated the room. Catherine turned the lights off in the kitchen.

"What's your name, hun?" asked Whitney, sitting on the floor beside her. Shaw stood above her, and I jumped up onto the back of the couch.

"Val Hayes, Special Agent. Federal Bureau of Investigation ." She kept her eyes closed and moved her legs to a more comfortable position.

"What year is it, Val?"

"Ah, 19… 20…2024."

"That's right."

"Can I have some water?" Shaw had already prepared a glass of fresh water and handed it to her as she sat up.

"Take it slow," Whitney told her, helping her into a more or less upright position. She reached out for the glass.

"What's the last thing you remember, Miss Hayes?"

She sipped the water and gave it back to Shaw, then rested her head on the cushion. "I remember taking off my seatbelt. Reaching for my weapon." Whitney made eye contact with Shaw.

"And then?"

She thought for a moment. "I don't think I remember." She put her hand to her side. "Wait, where's my handgun?" She patted her side again.

Shaw knelt down by her head. "It's probably still in your car." Shaw tilted his head up to Catherine. She nodded and went to check if it was in her jacket. "Miss Hayes, I'm Detective William Shaw, Copper Summit PD. This is Nurse Whitney Porter. You're in my house, the roads are impassable for the time being. I was involved in a vehicular accident with you a few hours ago. Do you remember who you were chasing?"

Val held her head and tried to think.

"It was snowing," said Shaw. "The roads were very slick, and I believe we were both in pursuit of the same person. Dark SUV, shots were fired…"

Her eyes suddenly opened. "Yes! The Baer house! I was there…"

"Will, go easy," said Whitney.

"No, no, no, I'm fine," Val said as she sat up straighter. "But I'd love some coffee." Catherine immediately went to retrieve it. "Black, please."

As Whitney checked her eyes with a tiny flashlight, Val complied but kept talking. "It's the dealership. Dale Sharpe Cadillac. He's been on our radar for years, but the Bureau finally decided to put me on the inside. I actually sell cars there. Was Employee Of The Month for November." She laughed but immediately stopped when it turned into pain.

So, Val *did* have her own office at the dealership. That's where I saw her last. I tried to remember her expression when she saw Shaw's cruiser out front, but the snow was coming down too hard. Had she been relieved to see us? Or mad that the local police were about to destroy her case?

Catherine brought over a mug with a snowman on it and carefully handed it to Val. After a few sips, she settled back into the cushions. She looked up at me on the edge of the couch and stroked my back. I purred.

"Who's this little guy?"

Shaw said, "That's Buck. He's uhh, been helping me today." He chuckled. "So... they placed you on the inside. Why?"

"Let me see if I can run down the list. Motor vehicle theft. Theft from interstate shipment. Export of stolen property. Identity theft. And several others along the way. I think we can add attempted and first-degree murder to that list."

She tried to stand up but couldn't quite get to her feet. Shaw took the mug, and Whitney gently guided her back down.

"Whoa, hun, take it easy. You've just —"

"No, I have to get back. This still hasn't been reported..."

"You mean, what happened at the Baer house?" asked Shaw.

"Yes! It was difficult to drive in the snow, and I couldn't call it in, couldn't even put my belt on trying to keep the car straight..."

"CSPD knows about it. And they know about you, so now the FBI knows. Okay. So tell me what happened there. You followed someone to the Baer's?"

She nodded her head. "His name is Anatoli Zarzandyan. Real... real character. He's the muscle of the group."

"He was the one in the SUV?"

"Yes. There was a pretty heated discussion about how to handle Bernard's situation, and eventually, Toli just took things into his own hands."

"Meaning he set out to kill Bernard."

"Correct. Do you know if he's okay?"

Shaw reported that he was.

"Good. He's a good man. He doesn't know what he's mixed up in."

"That's what I thought. But why kill him?"

Val reached out for the cup that Shaw held, took another sip, and started again. "In a nutshell, the hauler guy, I don't know what you call them, the guy that drives the trailer with all the cars on ramps behind. Alec Popov, mid 50's, another Russian. Or Eastern European. Not sure. Even though Alec was in on everything, he decides one day that this isn't his thing anymore. Wants a new life. And tells Anatoli. The thing is, Toli wasn't having it. Then there was a lot of shouting in Russian, and I saw through the glass walls that they're starting to get rough with him, and I stand up. Casually, I walk into the hallway where they were leading him, and around the corner I see them taking him out through this door. Has a code lock on it, I've never been through it. They pushed him in and followed behind, and that was the last I saw of him. That was about a week ago. That was the first time I realized just how bad these guys were."

But wait a minute, I thought. If this was the same guy I saw, the one they dragged through the tunnels while I hid in the shadows, they were coming from the opposite direction. Unless... unless Popov ran. Ran through the tunnels, not knowing where he was going, until he reached the forest. He probably thought himself lucky. Until Toli or the other guy put a bullet in his head. Then, they took him back through the tunnels and dragged him to the waterfall. That was a long way. But they expected him to walk there.

"Did the Bureau know about Popov at that point?"

"They did. I let them know everything. But I was collecting evidence, so we didn't want to bust them yet."

"Got it."

"So now, they don't have a driver for the hauler. You ever see the inside of one of those things? Two gear shifts, all kinds of levers, it's pretty complicated."

"But Bernard knows how to drive it."

"He does. So he's told to load up some vehicles and take them to the docks. About a five-hour trip. He can make it back by that evening. Oh, and he's told not to tell his wife. He protests. He doesn't understand why Alec can't do it. Doesn't get why they're dropping cars off instead of picking them up. Anatoli, uh, applies some pressure, I guess you could say, and Bernard backs down. He makes the drop-off, but the rig breaks down on the way back."

"Wait, wait. Bernard told me that he was picking up cars, not dropping them off."

Val laughed. "Yeah. He was dropping them off to ship overseas and sell in the Baltics. So now *he* knows. He's aware of the whole operation now."

"So he's their only driver, at least for the time being. How often do they make a shipment?"

"Once a week."

"Alright. So once the hauler breaks down, what happens?"

"They send one of the Russian mechanics down there to basically hold a gun to Bernard's head so he doesn't start talking. They're stuck for a couple of nights while the rig's being fixed, but during that time, things start to go sideways at the dealership."

"Why's that?"

"*You* showed up."

CHAPTER 27

Back to the Office

Our visit to the dealership. It seemed like that was the event that started unraveling this ball of string.

"Why don't we let Val rest for a bit before we start back up with the questions," said Whitney.

But Shaw continued as if Whitney was not there. "Dale was nervous when I talked to him about Bernard. And Anatoli… he was *not* happy we were there."

"Right. He knew the house of cards was getting ready to fall." Val still held her head.

"I think it's in mid-tumble."

"So do I. Listen, was my cell phone in my jacket? Or my purse? Or is that in the car too?"

Catherine had seen it while she was searching for Valerie's weapon. She retrieved it from the pocket of her white jacket and brought it over to her, the screen lighting up as soon as she touched it. "Goodness," Catherine said. "I think you might have missed some calls."

Val took it from her and nodded. I could see from the back of the couch that she'd missed several calls, most from Charlotte Office, SAIC Roman.

"Excuse me," she said, standing. "I'll need to take this in another room."

Whitney touched her arm and tried to guide her back down, but Val wasn't as compliant anymore.

"I'm fine."

Shaw stepped up to them. "You can use my study. I'll show you."

I took this as my cue to leave. There were several things I needed to take care of in my office. I just didn't want to miss anything here. I reminded myself that maybe a hidden webcam or baby monitor might help me in the future. For now, however, I had to take my chances and get back to the office.

Neither Shaw nor Catherine saw me slip out through the cat door.

The front porch had now accumulated at least a foot of blown snow underneath the overhang, and it was not easy, or enjoyable, to push through. Again, short hops were the most effective way of navigating back to my office. This storm had brought in colder temperatures than I could ever remember up here in the mountains. When the wind blew, it was torturous, even with my thick coat. The icy snow pelted my face and fur. I did not envy the animals caught outside in this blizzard. If they hadn't found shelter by now, their very lives would be in danger. And yet, here I was, about to summon a few of them to my office. I would have to suggest an arrangement that made sense for them to brave such unforgiving weather.

My final pounce took me to my office door. I unlocked it, stepped inside, and shook myself from my head to the tip of my tail, snowflakes drifting this way and that. How warm it was in here, literally a cat's dream. I peeked around the corner of my large desk, and there he was, Mr. Tuttle, on his back in front of the fire on the braided rug. How he got *into* that position or how he was going to get *out* of it, I did not know. He looked content and unmoving. He snored slightly. Good. The less interaction I had with him at this moment, the better.

Ariella lived in the oak tree next to the shed and could keep an eye out from her nest to see if I needed her. When I did, I placed a sign on the door that read:

OMFD

Outgoing Message For Delivery. It was handwritten by me, with a black Sharpie on a fluorescent green piece of posterboard. Hard for Ariella to miss, even 75 feet up in her tree. I rapped on the glass. Within minutes, there was a pecking at my door. I rushed to open it, not wanting to wake Mr. Tuttle otherwise I'd be engaged in an unending, mostly pointless, conversation.

A bit of wind and flakes flew into the office as I ushered her in, quickly stepping back so she would be less afraid of me and putting my paw to my mouth, indicating that she should be quiet. I went behind my desk to give her an adequate safety space from which to operate. She mostly closed the door with her beak but kept it open just a crack. She did not move forward and kept close to the door. For safety reasons.

"Ariella, I promise you're fine. I know most c-c-c-cats…. Most cats would like to c-c-c-catch a bird like you, but I… all I need is for you to deliver an important c-c-c-communiqué… for me…" I knew my tail was twitching. There was literally nothing I could do to stop it. That's how cats were wired. I knew it, and so did she.

"The weather's horrible, I know, and I'm sorry. I'm able to triple your rate of one worm to three, and I think I have some shiny things here in my desk drawer, they're yours. Is that good?"

She stepped forward furtively and craned her neck over my desk to look at my treasures. I placed two silver sequins from a vintage 1960s dress on my desk, which sparkled in the light from the hearth. Her eyes widened as I turned them back and forth in the firelight.

"Yes?" I asked.

She nodded her head, then stepped back toward the door.

"Okay then. I need you to please get in touch with Mr. Plankk again, the vole with the Picasso, but I'd like you to eat at least two worms before your flight. On me. You're going to need the protein."

She bobbed her head up and down.

"You remember where he lives?"

She nodded.

"Excellent. The letter says I'll need him here within 24 hours. It will take some time, and he will be well compensated."

Another nod. I threw two worms out the front door as I held it open for her, and she hopped away, picking up both worms from the snow at once and flying into the storm. I lost sight of her in a second.

CHAPTER 28

Into the Shed

With Ariella on her way, I quietly stepped back inside and slowly closed the door. Mr. Tuttle was still asleep on his back in front of the fire, and I gingerly put some more wood on what was already burning.

My earlier dream in the front seat of Shaw's Suburban had crystallized two things in my mind. The first was that there was indeed a body at the bottom of the waterfall, which had to be identified. If my plan worked, that crime would hopefully be solved by Mr. Plankk and the plumber, Hamilton Waters. The second was the beer can. Lev had one in his hands when he stood in the Shaw's shed but did not have it when he drove out to the tunnels. That meant he must have left it somewhere in the shed. Could there be prints on it? I didn't know. Could that prove to Shaw that someone other than himself had been in the shed? I didn't know that either. Getting Shaw out to the shed to even show him would be difficult. But I was taking things one step at a time.

So I sat down at my desk and typed an email to Mr. Waters. I pulled the chain on my green banker's lamp, brought my laptop toward the edge of the desk, and began.

Dear Mr. Waters,

You come highly recommended by Mr. Tuttle, a turtle with whom I believe you are acquainted. I wish to procure your services for a matter that is of the utmost importance. It does not require plumbing of any kind. However, it will require complete discretion, a few minute's dive into the frigid waters below the waterfall where Mr. Tuttle's house used to be, and a trip to 1028 Forest Hill Drive immediately upon completion. This is a matter of urgency, I'm afraid, and you will be compensated thrice your rate for an emergency job. Please allow me to briefly explain:

I was witness to an apparent murder or at least the disposal of a murdered body. This body is now somewhere underwater in the vicinity of the waterfall. I need you to find it, get a good look at the face, and travel to the above address. There will be a shed behind the house. You will find my office there, as well as payment for your services rendered.

Again, Mr. Waters, all this information is strictly confidential and needs immediate attention. Please respond as soon as you are able. I thank you for your swift reply and understanding of this delicate matter.

Yours Truly,
B. Buckleberry
Black Cat Detective Agency

I hit send.

Now, I only had one more thing to do — look in the shed for the beer can, which I assumed Lev had left there.

I pushed the laptop back and jumped down from my leather chair. The small gap between my ceiling and the shed floor started as a tiny crack, but with the unevenness of the floor above, it eventually became a few inches wide. I wasn't sure if I'd be able to slip through. If not, I'd have to come up with another way in. Carefully stepping past Mr. Tuttle, I climbed onto the first bookcase shelf in the corner of my office. The wood creaked. I stopped immediately and looked back at Mr. Tuttle.

He snorted and gasped, shook his tiny head, but then, with a sigh, went back to sleep. He started to snore as one of his feet shook gently, which made his shell turn in a slow circle. I waited a moment to make sure he was indeed asleep and then continued up the bookcase.

The crack at the very edge near the exterior wall produced the widest gap. I started to push my head through, not sure if I'd be able to fit or not. But when my whiskers didn't touch the sides and cleared the gap, I knew it would work. It would be tight, but I could make it.

I wriggled my way into the hole and into the cold darkness of the equipment shed above. The wind gusted outside, and I felt a draft through the spaces in the wood. I shook my fur, clearing it of dust and cobwebs, and sat there until my eyes adjusted to the dark.

First, I looked along the ground. There were boxes and containers and paint cans and lots of dust. No beer can. I jumped up to the first shelf. More of the same, along with some power tools and the occasional screw or bolt. But then, on the second shelf, I saw it.

It was a can of Coors Light, old with a faded logo and spots of rust. The can had been shoved behind an old cardboard box, like it was intentionally hidden. That seemed odd. With my paw, I teased it out of its spot until it fell over, rolled, and then dropped to the floor with a loud thunk. Oh no, I thought, would that wake Mr. Tuttle? I waited a few moments. The can sounded full when it hit the floor. I jumped down after it.

In the dim light that filtered through the wooden slats, I could see that the can had indeed been opened. In fact, looking at the top, it was an old pull tab, not the type you see now. The can must have been at least 20 years old. None of this made any sense. I spun it with my paw. Not for fun. For investigative purposes.

Something sparkled inside.

Bending down to get a closer look, I couldn't believe what I was seeing. I nudged the can with my nose until it rested in line with the crack at the front double doors so whatever light remained outside would shine directly into the old can. I looked in again.

Diamonds. The can was filled with diamonds.

CHAPTER 29

Power

Something must have been holding the diamonds together because I rolled the can for a little while, tumbling it back and forth, watching them sparkle on the inside, and they didn't rattle or spill out. I wondered how much they were worth.

The snow was still coming down harder than ever, and now, with evening approaching, everything outside was the shade of a dark ocean. I left the can on the floor of the shed and squeezed through the crack to get back into my office. Mr. Tuttle was still snoring. A perfect opportunity to check for a reply from Hamilton Waters. I stepped around my desk to my open laptop. I had mail.

Mr. Waters had indeed replied. With one word:

Understood

Did that mean he was diving into the waterfall now? Would he wait until morning? When would he be here? Was he okay with the payment offered? I had so many questions, but I guess I wouldn't have answers until he arrived. I hated one-word replies.

I closed the laptop and silently snuck out to the house.

Shaw, Catherine, and Whitney were finishing their coffee at the kitchen table. Catherine gave me a small bowl of cat food with obviously minimal effort. I forgave her, though, as there were currently more important things to worry about. Curled up under the kitchen window, I listened to their conversation.

"If the FBI knew about all this, why didn't they let you know?" asked Catherine. "I mean, Copper Summit Police?"

"They're not obligated to. The fewer people that know, the better, honestly."

"Yes, but couldn't you help?"

"They don't want our help, hun, they're the FBI."

Suddenly, the kitchen went dark. I looked up, expecting to see Patrick or Frannie next to the light switch, laughing. But no one was there.

"Oh, dear," said Whitney. "Was that the power?"

It obviously was. Even I knew that.

The fireplace filled the rooms with a dim, flickering light. With the exception of Shaw's office, the entire first floor was an open floor plan.

Shaw stood. "Guess it was. I figured that might happen sooner or later. Whitney, could you check in on Val? I'll put some more wood on the fire. Cath, can you get the flashlights and candles?"

Shaw was prepared for situations like this, and Catherine knew everything they needed was within easy reach. I got up and stretched, grateful for the few hours of relative relaxation I'd just had. Something told me that rest would come in handy.

The kids ran down the stairs, Patrick yelling, "Dad! Dad!"

"I know. It's fine. You two help your mother with whatever she needs. And stay out of the refrigerator!"

"Dad, can I help you start the generator?" asked Patrick.

"Not yet. If the power doesn't come back on in a bit, we'll start thinking about that."

"Aww, Dad!"

"Help your mother."

Val closed the door to Shaw's small study at the corner of the house and walked through the living room. "Power outage, huh?"

"Looks like it," said Shaw.

As Val came closer, she lightly grabbed Shaw's arm and quietly asked, "Detective, may I talk to you for a minute?"

"It's William. Or Shaw. And yes, of course."

They walked to the corner of the dining room, toward the back of the house. I went with them and brushed up against Shaw's leg, acting as innocent as possible.

"There's been quite a bit of action down in Charlotte," Val said.

"How so?"

"They were getting ready to mobilize when this storm moved in. They want to get a chopper up but can't fly in this weather."

"You already have enough against them to make some arrests?" Shaw raised his eyebrows.

"Hard evidence of ID theft, vehicle theft, and export. It's a little more sketchy on the Popov disappearance."

"The guy who was supposed to drive the hauler?"

"Correct."

"And they don't want to wait until you can get evidence of, what, murder?"

Val nodded her head. "That's what I'm thinking. These guys play hardball. But I'm pretty sure we'd have to get through that locked door in the dealership to find anything worth admitting into evidence. We don't have a warrant, and I don't see much happening in this storm. We'll have to wait it out."

"*You* don't have a warrant. If you give me probable cause to obtain one, I could talk to one of the judges here and see what he says."

Val hesitated. "You know, they drill into us to 'compartmentalize'. The Bureau does not like to share."

"Look. We've got one of these guys, Anatoli, dead to rights. I saw him try to take out Bernard."

"But did you?"

"Well, *you* followed him and saw him try to take out Bernard. That weapon he fired, it's an AK-12. I guarantee you no one within a hundred miles of this town has one. It's Russian military. We'll grab a few bullets from the couch and the wall, and I'll bet my house they'll be 5.45. There's your evidence. This guy's loose on my streets. That's enough to get a judge to sign off on a warrant."

"Sure. The ballistics can match up. But we need Anatoli. With the gun."

"In the Conservatory."

Val smirked. "Well, at least, in the Dealership."

"Alright. Deal then? I call my judge?"

Val put her head in her hands and ran her fingers over her face. "Fine. But I'm calling this in. I'll let them know that you're hellbent on getting this guy, and after what he did to the Baer's place, I can't stop you."

"You two," called Catherine from the kitchen. "Come and get something to eat." This was something she called a 'casserole'. I didn't know what was in a casserole or how to make one. But luckily, it was just about done cooking before the power went out.

I took a few bites of dry food from my bowl, which I'm sure was better than something called a 'casserole'. Sometimes human food can be disgusting.

While everyone finished eating, I rested in front of the fire. Honestly, there's no better place to be, especially during a snowstorm with a power outage.

There was a knock at the door. In the flickering light from the fireplace, everyone looked at each other. Patrick ran to the door, but Shaw loudly said, "No," and held his hand up. "I got it, son. Get back." Patrick looked at his dad, then went to stand by his mom in the kitchen. Shaw cautiously walked to the front door, and I followed close behind. There wasn't enough light to see who it was through the window, but when Shaw opened the door, a deep red firelight danced over Lev's ugly, rugged face.

PART THREE
DEALERSHIP

CHAPTER 30

Lev

In one motion, Shaw's right hand went to his hip, thumb sliding against the button that kept his revolver safe and in place on his holster. The thumb unlatched the strip of leather, and his hand closed on the grip, withdrawing the weapon in one smooth sweep, all taking place in less than a second. He steadied the revolver with his other hand and took a step back, pointing the weapon at Lev's chest.

"Get on the ground!" Shaw yelled. Lev put his hands up. His staunch expression didn't change. There was ice forming on his hair, and his thick eyebrows were frosted. He stared at Shaw, unmoving.

Shaw motioned, waving his gun down toward the snow-covered floor of the porch. "I said down!"

Slowly, Lev buckled his knees, arms still up, maintaining eye contact with Shaw while he knelt on the ground. He instinctively put his hands behind his head.

I watched from the front door as Shaw stood there for a second, unsure what to do. There was no car in the drive, only the Suburban and the police cruiser. Did he walk here? He must have. From where? I wondered if Shaw thought the same thing as he looked around the front yard in the fading light. It was almost dark now, but on the porch, it seemed the only light was from the reflection coming off the snow.

"Catherine!" he yelled, not taking his eyes off Lev.

"Here," she said. I looked up. She was holding a double-barreled shotgun, its black holes as wide as quarters, aimed at Lev's head.

"Eaaaasy," said Shaw. "It's okay, Cath, you can lower it." She hesitated, then slowly let the shotgun fall to her side. "I'm going to need to take him in. Get my jacket."

She left to get it.

Shaw kept his revolver trained on Lev. "Patrick!"

In a moment, he was there, excited to help. "Whoa…" he said as he looked at Lev.

"Never mind him. Mom's getting my jacket. Get the keys out of it, go out the back door, and start the Suburban."

"K, Dad!" He was off like a shot.

Shaw stood on the porch, not saying a word. Lev was silent as well. I stepped onto the porch as Shaw reached behind himself and softly closed the front door. All we could hear was the wind blowing through the trees and the tick of the frozen snow hitting the house.

"I don't know why you're here or what you're doing. I'm taking you down to the station. Why did you come here?"

Lev just grunted. A gust of wind blew snow onto the porch like a wave, curling around us, making an already cold situation almost unbearable. The front door opened, and Catherine appeared, holding Shaw's jacket. She put it down next to the door.

"Patrick's got the keys," she said.

"Okay. Still have the shotgun?" asked Shaw, keeping his eyes on Lev.

"I do."

"Pump it."

She chambered a round and put the stock up against her shoulder, pointing the barrels at Lev's chest.

"Do. Not. Move," Shaw said, looking at Lev a moment longer before he turned to grab his jacket. He shrugged himself into it, transferring the revolver from one hand to the other. Once it was on, he reached up and took the handheld mic from his shoulder.

"84 to Central. Bringing in Lev Luzhkov."

After no response for a few seconds, he repeated himself. Still, nothing but a click of static.

Shaw put the mic back and resumed his position, pointing his revolver at Lev with both hands.

Patrick ran from behind the house and to the front door of the Suburban. He slid into the front seat, and we heard the engine roar to life, the headlights instantly illuminating the falling snow. He stepped out and stood in the snow, looking toward us on the porch.

"The back door, on this side, open it please, Patrick."

He acted like a trained deputy and opened the back door.

"Go back inside. Thank you, bud."

Patrick ran out of sight to the back door.

Shaw made sure Catherine was still at the ready with the shotgun. He turned back to Lev. "Now I'm going to cuff you. Do not move."

I didn't know if Lev understood, and I'm sure Shaw felt the same way. He holstered his weapon and stepped around behind him. He took both hands in his and guided them down to his waist, but with Lev's thick jacket and the bulk of his body, his wrists would not come together. Shaw tried several times but eventually gave up and brought Lev's arms to the front. There, he speed-cuffed him with his hands in front, making sure they were tightly secured.

"That'll have to do. Get up."

When Lev did not comply, Shaw repeated the command and pulled up on the chain. Lev stood.

"I'm patting you down. Again. Do not move. Honey, point that thing at his head, away from his body."

When Catherine swung the weapon to Lev's head, Shaw ducked and began his pat down. Eventually, he was satisfied.

"Walk." With a little shove to Lev's back, he understood and walked through the snow down the slippery stairs. Shaw withdrew his .38 and kept it trained on Lev's back, and walked a step behind him. I ran past them, hopped up into the open back door of the Suburban, and scampered into the front. Shaw was too busy keeping an eye on the back of Lev's head to notice that I'd even hopped in.

When they got to the open back door, Shaw pushed Lev's head down and pushed him toward the back. Lev thought he was being put in the middle row, but Shaw quickly said, "Nope, all the way to the back," and made sure his body could fit through the narrow gap. Lev turned and sat.

"Try to keep safe back there. I'm not fool enough to reach in and put the seatbelt on you." He slammed the back door. He looked up to Catherine and now Val, both at the front door.

"I'm coming with you," said Val, pulling her jacket on.

"No. You're not. You're not ready for action, Val, sorry. Stay here and rest."

Her eyes shot daggers at Shaw.

"Cath, I'll call you," he yelled over the wind.

"But—" she started.

"It's one less thing for you to worry about."

Val retreated to the living room, and Catherine pushed the kids back inside. Patrick told his mom how cool all of this excitement was.

The driver's door opened, and Shaw slid in. He saw me on the seat.

"You've got to be kidding me."

I smiled and closed my eyes slowly at him.

"You… you are a stubborn cat, Beckett Buckleberry."

I couldn't have agreed more.

As we pulled out, the old Suburban tried to grab at the snow. Finally, with a hitch, we were off. The roads were just as bad, if not worse than when we were last out. I kept my paws on the front dash, looking between Shaw, the snow outside the windshield, and our prisoner in the very back.

Usually, Shaw talked to me now and then, but the storm was blowing the snow so hard that it made the vehicle difficult to control. He kept quiet and kept his eyes on the road, occasionally glancing to the back seat to make sure Lev had stayed put.

We rode in silence. Until a few miles down the road, we heard a deep voice growling from the back.

"Can I… trust you?"

Shaw looked into the rear-view mirror at Lev, speechless.

"I need help. Your help."

CHAPTER 31

Lev Talks

"So. You understand English now."

"*Nemnouga*. A little." He shifted in his seat, trying to situate his large body comfortably.

"Then you understand you perjured yourself back in Charlotte."

"Per-jer. I do not know this word."

Shaw's shoulder radio crackled. "82 to 84, come in Shaw." It was Alvarez.

He pulled the mic down and spoke. "Here, Jay. You're not gonna believe this."

"Well, you'll have a hard time believing this too..." A burst of static made Jay's next few words unintelligible. "Rafferty signed off on the…" More static. "…even there three minutes before it was signed and…" He cut out again. "…my way to the dealership…"

"Jay, look, if you can hear me, hold off a few. I've got Luzhkov in custody, and I'm taking him down to a cell for the time being. I'll go with you."

"What? How?"

"He, ahh, knocked on my front door." Shaw looked back to check on Lev, who was still in the same awkward position. There was no response from Jay. "You there?"

"Here, I…" His voice was drowned out again. It seemed like the storm was messing with the transmission.

"Jay, you're breaking up, but we'll get it figured out. And it seems our friend can actually speak a little English."

"Not the good English," said Lev from the back.

"…pulling into…wait in the cruiser… looks dark…"

"Just sit tight. Dropping off Lev at the station. I won't be long. 84 out." Shaw put the mic back on his shoulder. He lifted his eyes quickly to look at Lev in the rear-view. "So. You wanna tell me what's going on?"

"What is going on?"

"Yes. As in, why did you show up on my doorstep in the middle of a snowstorm."

"Am I under the arrest?"

"No. Not yet. I'm just taking you to the station so I know where you are. I don't want you near my family. Of course, you understand."

Lev nodded and grunted softly. "I did not mean to scare."

"Look. You're not under arrest, but I have lots of questions. Last time, you were let off on a technicality. That's not going to happen this time. Once we get to the station, if you want a lawyer, one will be provided to you."

Lev scoffed. "Bah. No lawyer. I only want help. For son. Mikhail."

"Your son's here?" asked Shaw.

"Da, in America."

"I mean, here, in North Carolina?"

"Da. That is what I said."

Shaw must have read the same thing I did, the INTERPOL file on the killer who sat eight feet behind us.

"Is that why you escaped Russia and came here? To find your son?"

"Mikhail was with me. Until you arrest me."

"In Raleigh?"

Lev turned his head to look out the window. "Da."

"Okay. And where is your son now?" Shaw kept darting his eyes to the rear-view mirror, but with the darkness setting in, Lev was only a black hulk sitting in the back seat.

"The Dale Sharpe. The Cadillac."

"He works there?"

Lev started to chuckle in the back seat. "Work. He is forced to work, he is… pris, how you say…"

"Prisoner?"

"Da. Prisoner."

The strings were starting to come together. Anatoli, an Armenian mob enforcer. Lev, a rising figure in the Balkan crime syndicate until he absconded with an unknown amount of jewels meant for Anatoli. Probably enough to fit inside an empty can of Coors from the '90s. So, Lev takes the jewels. Anatoli takes Mikhail.

A burst of static filled the silence. "Shaw! Come in!" It was Jay, and he was under duress.

Shaw quickly grabbed the mic from his shoulder, but before he could respond, the crack of gunshots cut through the static, and Jay was cursing before the radio went silent.

"Jay!" He waited a few seconds and repeated himself. Nothing.

CHAPTER 32

Firefight

If I thought Shaw had been taking the roads at an unreasonable speed earlier, now my concern was doubled. The wind blew us out of the few tracks he'd found in the road, and when it did, even with 4WD engaged, we slipped and slid. Lev bounced around in the back seat, at the mercy of Shaw's driving.

It took about ten minutes, windshield wipers on high, to make it to Dale Sharpe Cadillac. There were no interior lights on, and the sign was not lit. Neither were the sodium lamps in the parking lot. The glass building reflected the falling snow and the dimness of the fading winter light. Shaw pulled into the top of the lot, his headlights shining on Alvarez's cruiser. There were several bullet holes torn into the hood and driver's door. The passenger door was open, but Jay was nowhere to be found. Shaw put the Suburban into park. He turned back to Lev.

"Do not leave this vehicle. Do you understand me?"

"Da. Stay. Like dog."

"It's for your own protection. Do not leave."

"Detective," said Lev solemnly. Shaw turned his head back. "I do not leave car. You, you do not leave my son."

"Mikhail."

"Young. Built like young mule. Yellow hairs."

"Blond then."

Lev nodded. "Blond."

Shaw turned back, and was about to open the car door. He sat for a moment, then turned off the headlights and reversed to the edge of the lot, parked at an angle, out near the tall unlit sign by the road. Then he removed his gloves and threw them on the passenger seat, leaving the Suburban running.

Opening the door, he stepped out, zipped up his jacket, and withdrew his sidearm. I jumped out into the snow, already deep enough to cover my entire body. Shaw did not bend to pick me up but ducked behind the engine block, surveying the interior of the dealership. He closed the door quietly.

There were footprints in the snow from the driver's door of his partner's vehicle back to the trunk. He must have continued around to the passenger side to return fire from the open door. But still no sign of Alvarez. Thankfully, there was no blood.

A single shot lit up the interior of the dealership with a bright flash. After a second or two, there was a return fire from the opposite end of the building. Alvarez must be inside. But which side? In the next moment, at least two, possibly three, high-powered weapons discharged on the far left side of the showroom in short bursts. Alvarez must be on the right.

"84 to Central, come in." Shaw let up on the transmitter, but there was no response. "84 to Central, shots fired at Sharpe Cadillac. Officer Alvarez is inside. Send backup immediately, I'm going in." Shaw waited for an answer but did not receive one.

Crouching behind the hood and front tire, Shaw reached into his inside jacket pocket and pulled out his cell phone. He looked at the top corner. There were no bars, just the words "NO SERVICE." Shaw sighed and replaced the phone.

As he remained hunched over, I followed him and trotted behind the Suburban. He approached the window where Lev sat, and motioned downward with his hand. Lev understood and lay down on the back seat.

A huge concrete base supported the Dale Sharpe Cadillac sign, and Shaw ran to take cover behind it. I followed, settling next to him.

"Buck, you are a stupid, stubborn cat. Just do not get in my way."

I looked up at him, wishing there was a way to tell him what I knew. Even if there were, now wouldn't be the time. Instead, I hopped behind him as he ran for the trees on the right, which surrounded the property on three sides.

More shots rang out inside the building.

Shaw made it to the cover of a large oak, about 30 yards from the showroom. I hoped we were completely hidden within the cover of the copse of trees. Shaw looked to his right.

Just beyond the dumpster where we found the discarded files, a man walked slowly along the right side of the building. He wore a dark ski mask and carried an assault rifle slung over his shoulder, finger near the trigger. Whoever it was, he was attempting to circle to the side, effectively flanking Alvarez's backside. Shaw raised his revolver. The armed man had to clear the dumpster before Shaw had an unobstructed shot to the chest. But once the man walked beyond the cinderblock of the backside of the building, there was only glass.

This meant, at this angle, a missed shot could possibly end up taking out Alvarez. Shaw had a very small window of opportunity.

A 30-yard shot with a revolver. In snow and wind. Not ideal. Yet Shaw exhaled and clustered three rounds in quick succession at the man with the AK-12, taking him down in a heap. I didn't see any rounds left behind in the cinderblock. Shaw quickly turned to the cover of the old oak and looked back at me, my ears pinned to my head. He whispered, "Not bad, huh, Buck?"

He risked a glance back toward the building from the cover of the tree. No more shooting. If there were a large number of hostiles inside, they would have rained automatic fire down on Alvarez. It didn't seem to be that way. Each burst of enemy fire was short and coordinated. Alvarez remained outmatched but not overwhelmed.

In fact, since there was no immediate return fire after Shaw's three shots, whoever was inside was probably wondering where those shots came from. But they'd be able to tell that it was small arms fire, which meant that the men shooting at Alvarez knew that backup had arrived for him. Alvarez's weapon was the same as Shaw's—standard police-issue Smith and Wesson revolver. This meant two things: whoever was inside the dealership shooting at Alvarez knew that a third party had arrived, which was probably not reinforcements for them. And secondly, Alvarez knew the sound of an S&W .38 since he carried one as well. He knew Shaw was here.

But the question remained, how to get to Alvarez?

The safest line of entry to the building was the long route — through the woods, behind the dumpster, around the back protected by cinderblock, and then hope to find entry somewhere at the rear of the building. Otherwise, he'd approach the front door entirely exposed by glass.

All was silent inside the dealership.

Shaw crouched and quickly crunched through the snow to the back of the green dumpster where all this started. I followed in his footsteps, glancing back to the safety of the Suburban.

CHAPTER 33

Service Bay

Shaw was, understandably, no longer concerned about me. I had hitched a ride, a stowaway, and whatever happened to me now was not within his control. He moved forward through the snow without looking back until he came to the body on the ground.

The man was dressed in mostly black fatigues and was lying on top of an ever-expanding pool of blood, which seeped into the snow. Shaw knelt next to his head and put two fingers to the shooter's throat. If the man was alive, Shaw gave no indication.

Shaw pulled the ski mask up over the man's face. I did not recognize him, nor did I think Shaw. Thick, square face, somewhat similar to Anatoli's, but not his. Perhaps another Armenian. Shaw moved to relieve the dead man of his rifle but then uttered a single word.

"Damn."

It looked like one of his shots had hit the AK-12, tearing into the black metal near the chamber. The gun was now useless.

He moved into a crouching position and made his way toward the exterior wall, out of sight from anyone inside.

I could not imagine a human being sustaining three rounds to the chest and surviving. I stepped back as the blood expanded and darkened the snow near my paws.

I took one last look behind me at the beauty of the falling snow, then turned toward the building, making a quick run for the side. In a few bounds, I made it. No shots fired.

In fact, with the exception of the soft patter of snow falling on the ground, it was as quiet as a church at midnight. Almost eerie.

Shaw was already at the back corner of the building, revolver out and at the ready. He quickly peered around the cinderblock, then relaxed his body a bit. It seemed that all was clear on that side. He cautiously turned the corner. I followed.

Immediately, we saw two sets of massive garage doors leading to the mechanics' bays. Shaw looked in through the long horizontal window, but it was too high for me to see anything. He peered, staring into the darkness.

As I looked for a way into the bay, I saw a small circle, a six-inch diameter hole in the garage door, covered with a piece of metal on a hinge. I pawed at it, watching it swing and creak with every swipe. This was my way in — a hole cut into the door for exhaust fumes from running cars while the bay door was closed. I batted at it again and put a paw on it to stop it from swinging. I put my head through, and the rest of my body followed. I heard Shaw move on, crunching through the snow.

The garage was huge but dark, even with the bank of horizontal windows. I held my position to let my eyes adjust, and slowly, things came into focus.

There were several bays inside, only a few of which held cars. I counted — eight bays on each side for a total of 16. With the electricity out, there was no heat. The concrete floor quickly added to the chill of the area, and my paws were painfully cold. I decided to keep moving.

No shots were fired since we took cover in the woods. Was anyone still alive? Were they regrouping? Changing positions?

I walked to the far side of the garage, but something stopped me in my tracks. A human moan and the clanking of metal. I dropped to the floor as soon as I heard it, eyes immediately expanding and ears pinned back. Low to the ground, I allowed a second or two to slip by, then rotated my ears forward, trying to ascertain the sound. Breathing, shallow and soft.

Was this Alvarez? Was he hurt?

Realizing I was exposed in the middle of the floor without any cover, I ran to a large red tool trolley on wheels and squeezed underneath. It gave me cover with a better vantage point than from the center of the garage. Now, I could see a man lying on the ground, halfway under the front of a late-model Cadillac, with at least one hand shackled to a large, almost medieval manacle. A chain led from his wrist, up over a workbench, and ended in a large steel plate mounted to the wall. Whoever he was, this man was a captive.

A shot rang out from beyond the walls of the garage. It seemed to be coming from inside, maybe from the main showroom. Perhaps Alvarez was still alive — that would be the only explanation for any shooting still going on unless Shaw had already made it into the showroom. Or, the injured man in front of me could be Alvarez. Both options were not ideal. Slowly, I scooted out from under the tool chest and approached the man as low to the ground as possible.

Now I could see he wore a dark mechanic's uniform, and his hair was light. Alvarez had dark hair. This was the young man that I'd seen Lev embrace in the woods by the tunnels. He was here. Lev's son, Mikhail. He was young with blond hair. He had a black eye and some blood dripping from his forehead. He opened his eyes and saw me. He smiled.

"Hey, kitty." He stretched out his hand to me. Did I trust him? Should I let him know that someone was here and that law enforcement was aware of what was going on? Of course, I couldn't tell him these things, but with a nudge of my head against his hand, perhaps that would lift his spirits. But I didn't want to be grabbed if I happened to be wrong. I'd be cautious.

I lifted one paw and started to make my way toward his outstretched hand. It took a few moments, but eventually, I reached him, and as his fingers spread outward to reach my head, I nuzzled against them, letting him know I trusted him. He petted my fur for a bit, and then his hand dropped to the ground as he lost consciousness once more.

I stepped back, watching his head slowly bleed onto the concrete floor. A large wrench with some blood on the edge lay close by. I thought someone must have wanted to keep him quiet, and a hard blow to the head accomplished just that.

A tapping. I heard it echo throughout the garage, sharp and persistent. I stepped out from under the car and looked around. It was coming from the huge bay door.

On the outside, perched on the thin strip of rubber that surrounded the entire horizontal window, was the dark silhouette of Ariella, pecking on the glass to get my attention.

CHAPTER 34

Oil Painting

"Ariella! What… how…" I ran to the roll-up door.

Pushing the little circular plate aside with my nose, I peeked my head out into the snow. And there she was, hovering, the wind blowing her up and down as she tried to keep her balance. And below her, looking quite tired and cold, were Mr. Plankk, the vole, and Hamilton Waters, the beaver plumber. I was shocked.

"You guys can't be here, this is… there's bad people here!"

Mr Plankk stood on his feet, holding his paws close to his chest, looking around warily while Mr. Waters shook his heavy coat free of accumulating snow.

"What are you doing here? Ariella, you were supposed to bring them to my office!" My head was halfway out of the exhaust hole when I suddenly realized it might be more dangerous for them outside than inside the quiet service area.

"She found us both, Mr. Buckleberry," said Mr. Plankk, high voice squeaking. "Me first, and then Hamilton. We were on our way to your office, but she spotted you from above and thought it might be a good idea to stop to talk here because of the storm. And possibly, get out of the weather."

"Fine, all of you, quickly…" I said as I waved them in.

Mr. Plankk easily scampered through the hole, followed by Ariella's short hop in. Hamilton Waters needed more help.

It seemed that only his head fit through the 6-inch hole, and the rest of his body simply would not budge. He groaned and struggled and tried wriggling through, back legs kicking wildly up in the air, but it was no use. Waters was not getting in.

"Hamilton," I told him, "I'm sorry, but if it's not too uncomfortable for you, I think we can conduct our business this way."

"What, with my hindquarters sticking out in the cold?"

"Yes, we don't have much choice," I answered.

He humphed. "Very well. But this is triple time, don't forget. Besides, I'm not going to be able to fix any plumbing issues confined like this."

"Again, this involves no plumbing. I just need you to tell Mr. Plankk what you saw at the bottom of the waterfall."

"This is all highly unusual," said Hamilton, front paws and slick, furred head sticking through the hole.

"Oh… oh dear…" whimpered Mr. Plankk. He had seen the young man lying on the ground.

"Ah. Yes. Him," I said. What could I tell them? Only Hamilton knew about half of what was going on, and even then, there was no way for him to connect the dots. And I had no idea why Lev's son was lying on the cement floor, injured and chained to a wall. So I told them the only thing I could.

"He's on the overnight shift. Decided to stay here to ride out the storm. Try to be quiet."

"Ohhh…" said Mr. Plankk.

"Now then. Mr. Plankk, I'm hoping, because of the Picasso you have hanging in your living room, that you have a great appreciation of art, do you not?"

"Oh, most certainly yes!"

I shushed him with a paw to my mouth.

He meekly repeated himself. "…most certainly yes…" he peeped.

"Very good. And you sketch things yourself? Meadows and flowers and other animals…"

"My wife is my very favorite subject. That's true."

"Then, I'm going to need those special skills of yours right now, Mr. Plankk. If we were in my office as originally planned, I would have provided you with paper and pencil. But as we're here, in the service area of a car dealership, we will have to improvise. Let's see what we can find."

"Okay, but what am I drawing?" Mr. Plankk asked.

"You are about to become the world's first Arvicolinae sketch artist."

"Oh my. Well, that does sound very important."

Hamilton raised his head. "He'll sketch who I saw underwater?"

"With your help, Mr. Waters, that's the plan. Mr. Plankk, Hamilton is an eyewitness to a body whom I believe to have been murdered. He, other than the killers themselves, is the only one who can accurately describe the victim. You'll sketch what he describes. But first, we'll need some artist's tools."

As Hamilton hung in the hole, flapping his clawed paws back and forth, Mr. Plankk and I examined the contents of the garage for whatever we could find. I didn't think there'd be paintbrushes or canvases here, but we could make do with other things if we were creative enough.

I pulled open several drawers on the tool chest I had previously hidden beneath as Mr. Plankk looked around on the ground for whatever he could find. He was careful to be as quiet as possible so as not to wake Mikhail, which was not very difficult at all for him.

I pulled out a drawer that contained a variety of wire wheels, discs and brushes with a hex end, which would attach to a drill to clear rust or debris from engine parts. I held up a small one, the brush end smaller than my paw. "Would this work?" I asked. The vole looked up.

"Oh, yes! What a wonderful paintbrush!"

I put my paw to my mouth again, and he meekly apologized, giving me a thumbs up. "But now we need paint," he said quietly.

We both scoured the garage. In the corner of the service bay was a small area where it looked like they did paint touch-ups after bodywork was completed. Unfortunately, there were only sealed cans of auto paint that were used with an air compressor and a paint gun. Between the four of us, I didn't think we'd be able to open the cans. I looked back at Mr. Plankk.

He was inspecting the bay next to mine, leaving little quarter-inch paw prints on the garage floor. He must have stepped in oil. Wait a minute, oil…

Under the vehicle that Mikhail was working on was a drip pan. I bounded over to it. There was our paint — a tray filled with dirty motor oil. I nosed it closer to Ariella and Hamilton and made a short hissing sound, gaining Mr. Plankk's attention. He looked up, then came running over.

"Oh, this is perfect," he said, "but what do I paint on?"

I gestured with my paw to the cement floor.

"Ah, yes! The dealership won't mind?" he asked.

"Not one bit. Mr. Waters, are you ready?"

Hamilton adjusted himself in the hole. "Yes. The sooner we can get this over with, the sooner I can get my front end out and warm my backend instead."

Ariella seemed excited, jumping from one foot to the next.

Mr. Plankk readied his brush, dipping the tip into the tray of used oil. He held it in his tiny paw and looked at the beaver, ready for instruction.

"Mr. Waters," I started. "How would you describe the man whom you saw at the bottom of the waterfall?"

The beaver thought for a moment and then said, "Dead."

I cleared my throat. "Yes. But his facial characteristics, did he have a round head? A square one?"

"I would say, maybe not either, but longer, like umm... who's that guy?" Hamilton seemed lost in thought and put a paw to his face. "The dolphin guy. He beat up Rocky."

"Like in a movie? A dolphin beat up Rocky?"

"Yes. Dolphin Green, Greenland Dolphin..."

I was utterly baffled. "That's his name?"

"Yes! Didn't you see it? One of the Rocky movies. 'If he dies, he dies.'"

"Dolph Lundgren? Rocky IV?" I guessed.

"That's the one." Hamilton pointed at me.

I asked Mr. Plankk if he knew who that was.

He smiled. "I love the Rocky movies, Mr. Buckleberry. I base my workout regimen on his."

I nodded. "Alright then. So he looks like Dolph Lundgren."

Mr. Plankk started to paint on the floor, stepping around his dark strokes as the brush kept working, then moving to the other side to continue the shape of the face. It was starting to come together.

"Yes," said Hamilton, "but much older. And bags under his eyes."

Mr. Plankk made the necessary adjustments, covering over his lines with new ones and adding strokes where there were none before.

"Oh yes, that's good," said Hamilton, craning his neck to look at the painting from a slightly different angle. "And his nose, it was much wider and flatter. I can see it now."

A brush stroke here, a dark line there, and the nose grew uglier.

"The chin, maybe it's a little more angular, like the bottom of a heart."

Mr. Plankk dipped the wire brush into more oil and painted on the floor, sharpening the chin, scampering back and forth as he smoothed the lines into the cheeks.

"Oh. Gosh. Yes. I think that's him," said Hamilton.

Mr. Plankk, Ariella, and I stepped to the bottom of the painting and looked at it. It was surprisingly realistic.

"It's like you took a picture of him," said the beaver.

"Thank you," said Mr. Plankk. "My wife sits for me sometimes and lets me practice sketching, though her face is more triangular…"

Gunshots broke the relative silence. Ariella shrieked and tried to get out the same way she came in, but a beaver was blocking her exit. Nevertheless, she bounced against him several times. When she realized that was not working, she flew into the rafters and hid in the farthest corner. Mr. Plankk dropped the dripping oil brush and scurried inside a tire lying on the ground. Hamilton pushed himself backward, grunting and groaning as he managed to move his bulk in the opposite direction, repeatedly saying "no, no, no, no…" until he was suddenly free and dropped to the snowy ground. The small circular door pivoted to a close behind him.

And me? I made my way toward the sounds of gunfire, looking for a way to get into the showroom itself.

CHAPTER 35

Into The Fire

The service bay was isolated from the dealership's main floor for obvious reasons — no one wanted to hear the cacophony of air hammers, pneumatic drills, and other unpleasant bangs and booms while shopping for a high-end vehicle. I'd searched and sniffed in corners for any exit with no luck.

There was a locked door to Parts, then another locked door, which likely led to offices and the showroom floor. There was also a vault-like institutional green door, massive and out-of-place, which was locked with a keypad. I had no idea where that led.

The only other door was a 20-foot roll-up, though this one was made of transparent plastic, which looked out over the service entrance. I assumed customers dropped their cars in that section before a technician lifted the door and brought each vehicle into the bay. But where was the switch to raise it?

There it was, to the right of the door, but too high to reach. Three oversized buttons in a steel box read UP, DOWN, and STOP.

If I could open the door, I could access the service entrance. But I'd still have to figure out how to get to the showroom.

The gunfire continued, sporadic popping cracks from the dealer floor. Why was I even headed in that direction? I should have just hidden far behind one of the vehicles here in the service bay, but Shaw was most likely in the main showroom, and if there were any way to help him, I would.

A circular padded stool on wheels sat next to one of the cars on the other side of the garage. Sprinting over to it, I nosed it along, inch by inch, until I was able to place it directly beneath the switch box for the door. I hopped up onto the cushion.

It spun as soon as I jumped onto it. I had to hold on with all four paws until it slowed down. I used one paw to touch the wall and bring it to a complete stop.

Every time I attempted to stand on the seat, the movement made the stool swivel again, so I had to hold onto the wall to steady myself. Now, I just had to make myself taller and longer until my left paw could touch the OPEN button. With a little effort, I finally reached it.

With a loud whirr, the entire door lifted, and in two seconds, the space was open, inviting an immediate hail of bullets that smashed against the wall two feet away. I jumped down, almost sliding off the stool, and ran, hiding around the corner. It was automatic fire. I knew Shaw had no such weapon, and I was almost certain that Alvarez was armed only with his service revolver. I hoped that didn't mean backup had arrived for whoever was returning fire.

As soon as the shooting stopped, I peered around the corner of the wall. I could make it to the side of a long desk in the service entrance if I ran low to the ground, and now was the best time to do it. I took off.

From the relative safety of the service counter, I looked out into the showroom. It was dark but not pitch-black. The snow outside dimly lit the interior, and I could see the ruin that the gunfight had produced.

The main vehicle on display in the showroom was a huge Escalade. Two of its tires were flat, and the windshield smashed. Jagged holes ripped through the sides.

Glass windows were shattered, allowing the snow and cold to drift inside. For the moment, all was quiet again, but it wouldn't last long.

The barrage of bullets that I had just avoided resulted in one good thing — a glass panel between the service department and the showroom was now shattered on the floor into a million pieces. I could get in.

Stepping around larger chunks of broken glass, more and more of the showroom became visible. I saw movement to my right — the dark outline of a man wearing a tactical vest carrying a long weapon. I instantly knew it was not Shaw or Alvarez, but he was advancing in their direction, close to the wall. I had to act.

I darted through the opening and meowed loudly as I brushed past the man's feet, intentionally rubbing against him. Sprinting to the safety of the destroyed Escalade, I slid underneath. He exclaimed something in Russian, then turned to fire at me, emptying a few rounds into the side of the vehicle. The muzzle flashes lit everything in bright orange.

From the other side of the showroom, with his revolver in both hands, Shaw took the man out with two quick shots. The man crumpled to the floor. Shaw instantly dropped behind the safety of a sleek CT4. Bullets from the other side pelted the car relentlessly.

More shooting filled the room, almost too loud for my ears to bear. I flattened them to my head and crawled to one of the blown-out tires, hiding as best I could. I couldn't see Shaw and Alvarez but knew where they were. At some point, I'd have to make a break for it and run half the length of the showroom to join them.

The shots were so loud that my ears were ringing. Glass crashed to the ground. I felt the hard pelting of rounds hitting the steel of the vehicle above me. Bullets ricocheted. This was not a safe place to be.

Then, in a moment of silence, it dawned on me. All of the gunfire now came from one side, the side where the man with the automatic weapon had appeared. There was no return fire from Shaw or Alvarez. In the eerie stillness, it was clear that Shaw and Alvarez were out of ammo.

CHAPTER 36

Showroom Floor

It seemed as if the gunfire would never stop. The car that Shaw and Alvarez hid behind was being shredded, and there was nowhere to run. If they left the cover of the CT4 and ran back through the smashed windows to the outside, they'd be fully exposed — black silhouettes against a field of white. They were trapped, and there was nothing I could do to help.

The loud growl of an engine came from outside, and then one of the last remaining glass panels exploded into the showroom in a blast of sparks and flying glass and metal as Shaw's Suburban crashed through the other side of the dealership. The sound was unbearable, the high shriek of the engine, glass, steel, and plastic being twisted and crushed as the SUV plowed through cars, workstations, and men. The gunfire was now trained on the Suburban, but it continued to smash forward. There were screams as bodies were run over or pushed into cars, the huge SUV destroying everything in its path until it came to rest at an upward angle, its front passenger tire tilted up onto the hood of a showroom car.

For a moment, all was quiet.

Shaw took advantage of the pause in fire and rushed out into the darkness to grab the weapon from the man he'd shot. Almost slipping in a pool of blood, he untethered the sling from the man's shoulder and wrapped the Russian AK-12 over his own. Alvarez came up to join him, and they quickly took cover near me in front of the Escalade. I rubbed against Shaw's leg as he knelt beside me, and his hand ran along my back.

There was a creak as the Suburban door opened.

Shaw felt confident enough to shine his Maglite in that direction. It drew no attention. Still, he was careful and approached the vehicle in a crouch, hiding behind the wreckage of cars as often as he could. Alvarez followed, and I followed Alvarez.

The flashlight revealed the extent of the damage. Not one square inch of the showroom was free of the remnants of glass or metal. A small fire glowed in the corner where something had ignited. They ignored it as we all moved carefully forward.

Alvarez stopped to pick up a handgun from a body on the floor. He turned the man over to search for a spare magazine, found one, put it in his pocket, and quietly laid the body back on the ground.

As we traversed the length of the ravaged showroom floor, Shaw and Alvarez stepped over a wooden frame, ignoring it. It was an Employee Of The Month plaque.

Looking over all the photos behind individual square glass panes, I recognized Val. November must have been a good month for her. Then, my eyes settled on Employee Of The Month for April —Alec Popov. The same face Mr. Plankk had drawn on the service bay floor. And the same face that now rested at the bottom of the Courtland County Strict Nature Reserve waterfall.

I pawed at the edge of the picture, teasing it out from under the broken glass. I managed to get a corner out and pulled it free with my teeth. I scampered to catch up with Shaw and Alvarez.

Shaw directed his partner to move to the other side of the showroom floor, effectively flanking whoever might still be alive on the opposite end. Ultimately, there was no need to — every body they came across had no pulse. They checked behind upturned desks, behind ruined vehicles, underneath fallen cubicle dividers. Only then did they make their way to the upended Suburban.

Lev sat in the driver's seat and smiled at Shaw as he approached.

"Thought I told you to stay put."

"You are welcome," Lev said, holding his side and groaning. Blood spilled from between his fingers.

"Dammit. Jay, come here."

The Maglite showed the damage to Lev's midsection. Based on the amount of visible blood, it was probably a deep wound. But carefully peeling his jacket back revealed much more than a stray bullet. A piece of metal a few inches long protruded from Lev's stomach.

"Not good, yes?" Lev asked.

"Correct," said Shaw. "Not good."

"My son. He is here. I must leave with him."

Jay had found a promotional T-shirt near one of the cubicles and handed it to Shaw.

"You need to stay here. Hold this to your wound. Do you understand?" Shaw unlocked the handcuffs that Lev was still in, then placed the shirt into his midsection. Lev winced. He nodded and took the shirt, pressing it into the wound.

"Help is coming," said Alvarez.

Lev chuckled. "Help is not coming."

"We'll see. But you have to stay here."

Lev shook his head. "No. I will find Mikhail. He is here."

Shaw exhaled. "Look. I'm not going to cuff you to the wheel. You do what you need to do. But you'll die if you keep moving around."

Lev nodded. "Yes."

Shaw looked down at me and saw what was in my mouth. He bent down.

"So what did you manage to find, Buck?" I opened my mouth and let him take the picture. He shone his light on it. "Who's this?" Jay looked over his shoulder but didn't recognize him either. Shaw showed the picture to Lev.

Lev nodded. "Popov. He… he helped me to find son. Good man."

"Alec Popov?" said Shaw. Lev nodded again. The original vehicle hauler who wanted out. Who was, according to Special Agent Valerie Hayes, shoved through a heavy, locked door with a passcode box on the side and never heard from again.

"Buck," said Shaw, bending down to me again. "How did you…"

But his sentence was cut short as more gunfire erupted from the back hallway off the rear of the showroom. I ran for cover as Shaw flattened himself on the ground and Alvarez slid under the Suburban. After another short burst of shots, we heard the distant sounds of running footsteps and Russian words, spoken in a hurry, echoing from the hallway. A moment passed, and Shaw stood as Alvarez peered out, confirming all was clear.

"What did they say?" Shaw asked Lev urgently.

Lev was losing the color in his face. He lifted his head a bit. "Tunnels…"

CHAPTER 37

Tunnels

We left the safety of the hulk of Shaw's old Suburban and made our way to the administrative offices.

A loud metal clang filled the dark hallway. We ran toward the sound.

I became painfully aware that I had glass stuck in my paws, and I could feel it with every step. Not large pieces, but tiny shards that would probably be difficult to remove with my teeth. If I survived, Catherine or Dr. Wells would have quite a time with me.

Shaw's Maglite beam bounced up and down the walls as we ran. Up ahead, the hall came to a T, and after a brief pause, Shaw turned right. At the end of the hall was a green door, similar to the one I'd seen in the service bay but not nearly as wide. It wasn't just a door. It looked like the opening to a vault—similar to the one in the garage bay, but much smaller. A lit keypad was set into the wall. There was no way we were getting through that door without the code. We came to a standstill.

"Think we can hot-wire it?" asked Alvarez.

Shaw looked at him a second before answering. "Jay. This isn't the movies." He shone the light on the buttons, inspecting the keypad more closely.

"What is it?" Jay leaned his head forward.

"Blood. Light traces, but it's there. On the 1, 2, and 4."

"It's fresh?"

Shaw wiped at one button with the tip of his finger. "Yes."

"Well, there you go. So, what's our next move?"

"I don't know. I wouldn't think the code would be three digits. Right? Not for a door like this…"

"Agreed."

"So it's some combination of them. Any of those numbers mean anything to you?"

"No," Jay replied. "They're getting away."

"I know. But at least one of them is injured."

"What about an area code?"

"If so, it wouldn't be from around here," Shaw answered.

As they talked about different combinations of codes, I sat down and tried to bite away some of the glass from my paws. The ones on my pads were easier than the ones stuck deep between them. I'd have to deal with those later.

I had an idea about the code, but I had no way to communicate it unless…

Getting back on my feet, feeling the sting with each step, I headed down the hallway in the opposite direction. Once I turned the corner, I no longer had the indirect light from the Maglite beam. But as I made my way through the hall, the soft orange glow of the fire that had started on the showroom floor flickered over the walls.

I wondered if it would eventually burn itself out or the opposite — start a much bigger conflagration.

One of these offices had to be unlocked. I nudged each door until one swung open, allowing me to enter.

Surrounded by darkness, I gave my eyes a few seconds to adjust. It felt like an eternity, and as soon as I could see, I jumped onto Sales Manager Matthew Mason's desk (at least that's what his nameplate stated) to find what I was looking for.

In the far corner beside his phone was a pile of brochures for Dale Sharpe Cadillac, with a picture of the building on the cover. And in the bottom right-hand corner of the brochure was the phone number, website, and physical address — 2412 South Trail Vista Drive.

I swiped the brochure off the desk, grabbed it with my mouth, and dragged it back to Shaw and Alvarez.

When I returned, they were still contemplating possible combinations, how many digits the most reasonable code contained, and whether the system would lock them out after so many attempts. I dropped the brochure on the floor.

Shaw picked it up, looking over to me. He perused the cover, thought for a moment, and punched in 2412, followed by a button at the bottom marked OPEN. Nothing but an error beep.

"What are you doing?" Alvarez asked.

"Look at the address," he said, pointing.

"Okay. Try it backwards."

Shaw did. Still, nothing.

"Let's try twice," Shaw said, but doubling the number resulted in another error code.

"Maybe this…" Shaw input 24122142, the address forward and backward. The keypad lit green, and the bolts around the door snapped back with a bang. The two men exchanged a look of surprise. Shaw pulled on the handle, and the heavy door slowly opened to a dark, downward steel staircase.

Shaw lit the way as we carefully navigated the long stairs, not knowing what waited at the bottom. But when we got to the end, it was just a dirt floor and a narrow path forward.

The tunnel was lit by fluorescent tubing set high up into the rock. It wasn't long, maybe ten yards, before we came to a split. I was almost certain that if we took the opening to the right, it would lead us back to the green door I'd seen in the garage. And to Mikhail, who needed medical attention. But we also needed to follow the men who evaded us back in the showroom. I didn't know which was more important, but I knew Lev deserved to see his son, even if for one last moment. I stepped into the right-hand tunnel and meowed.

And meowed.

And meowed again.

"Fine, Buck, let's go," said Shaw, following me down the wide rocky corridor. He yelled to Alvarez, "Take the other tunnel, I'll catch up!" In an instant, Jay was gone around a curve, the Glock held tight in his right hand, heading toward who knew what.

The brighter lights in this portion of the tunnel allowed me to see tire tracks in the dirt. Were they in other parts of the tunnels as well? I had no idea. This portion of the tunnel was also more of a ramp. The incline was steady and steep enough that after a minute of walking, Shaw was starting to tire.

Just around a long, wide arc, we encountered the opposite side of the huge service bay door. There was a steel box that contained a single large round button. Shaw shooed me back behind him and quietly approached the door, lifting the AK he had taken from the dead man in the showroom. He made sure there was a round in the chamber, then pressed the red button.

The heavy locks clicked out of place, and the door swung forward. He peered through. There must not have been anything to see because he pushed against the heavy door and let it swing forward on its own weight.

He stepped through.

Walking into the garage, Shaw kept the AK-12 at the ready, sweeping it as he searched for any sign of activity. There was none. He held the Maglite underneath, and its beam found something on the floor.

Mr. Plankk's painting of Alec Popov.

"What the…" He stepped toward it, eyes narrowed. I have to say, whatever Mr. Plankk's profession was, he seriously could reconsider and move into portrait painting full-time. Shaw looked down at me.

"You know anything about this?" he asked.

In response, I mewed softly but stepped away from the painting and over to the car where I had left Mikhail.

Except, he was no longer there. The chain that had kept him hostage had been cut, and a greasy angle grinder sat on the garage floor next to the broken link. The blood from Mikhail's head was in a pool on the floor.

CHAPTER 38

Branches

Of course, Shaw had no idea that the broken shackle had once held Lev's son captive. He inspected the blood and chain quickly, took a cursory look around the garage, and then scolded me for leading him in the wrong direction.

"We're wasting time, Buck," he said as he ran back towards the tunnels. "Come on."

Something made a sound behind me, and I turned.

It was Rathbone Plankk peeking out of the overturned tire. His small nose sniffed the air.

"Stay there, Mr. Plankk, it's dangerous out here."

"I should say so," he squeaked, his eyes barely visible above the rubber rim of the tire.

With a flapping of wings, Ariella touched down right in front of me. I looked over my shoulder, but Shaw was already far down the tunnel.

"Look, you two, it's best if you either stay here out of the storm or try to make it home. I didn't mean for you to be involved in this, we were supposed to meet back at my office…"

Ariella cocked her head and scratched at the garage floor.

"I know. I owe you. I owe you both."

"Mr. Buckleberry? Are you leaving us here?" Mr. Plankk seemed scared, but his two clawed hands grabbed the rubber, and he showed me more of his furry head.

"Yes, I have to go help."

"What's going on?" he asked.

"Well, there seems to be a... small Soviet mob war going on, and we're in the middle of it."

"Oh, dear." He ducked his head again.

"Yes, but if you stay here, you'll be safe. And warmer than out there, at least."

"And if we come with you?" he asked. Ariella backed up and shook her head.

"If you come with me, perhaps you could help. But I can't guarantee your safety." I wondered if either of them had seen what happened to Mikhail. "Did you see what happened to the boy?"

Plankk popped up further from the edge of the tire. "The young man that was chained to the wall? We saw two men cut him loose with that power tool, they seemed... angry."

"There were two of them?" I asked. "Was one injured?"

"The bigger one's arm was bloody." Plankk crawled out of the tire and came closer to me, looking around to ensure it was safe.

"That's good information, Mr. Plankk, thank you. What else did you see?"

"Well, that was about it. They spoke in a different language, so I couldn't tell what they were saying. But I know they were mad."

"Did they call each other by names?"

"Not that I know of..."

"Did you hear the name 'Anatoli'?"

"Yes! That's what the smaller one called the bigger one!"

I looked back to the open tunnel doorway. I was running out of time, and even though I could run and catch up to Shaw, there were multiple branches that he could take. I had to hurry.

"I understand if you both want to stay here, but we could use all the help we could get. Maybe we can save that boy's life."

I didn't know how we'd be able to do that or how we could stop Anatoli from getting away. But I had to try.

Mr. Plankk hesitantly stepped forward. "Oh…oh…okay…" he said, barely audible.

"You'll come?"

He nodded.

"You are the bravest vole I've ever met, Mr. Plankk."

"I'm scared."

"I'm scared too. But that's what being brave is. Doing the right thing even when you're really, really scared."

Rathbone Plankk stood a little taller.

I looked over to Ariella. She shook her head and moved back even further.

"That's fine, Ariella. It's okay. Come on, Mr. Plankk."

We walked through the large green industrial door, and I took one last look back at Ariella. She was pecking at the ground nervously. Perhaps she was conflicted. I didn't know. I wasn't very good at interpreting bird behavior.

But a few minutes later, as we ran down the tunnel, we heard the flutter of wings. Without stopping, I looked up at the brave bird who flew two feet above us, following us down the rocky corridor.

We came to the stairs that led back up to the offices, and I stopped in my tracks. A deep red trail of blood led down to the tunnel floor, splashed over the stairs, still dripping. It was definitely not there when we descended. And there were no footprints in the dirt leading in the direction of the stairs, which meant someone had come down behind us.

Lev.

Ariella hovered, and Mr. Plankk sniffed the air while I inspected the blood trail.

"Gosh. That's a lot of blood," Plankk said anxiously.

I nodded. "We need to keep moving."

Once our team was on the move again, I turned to Mr. Plankk as we ran. Ariella fluttering above. "The blood, I think it's from Mikhail's father, Lev. He's very stubborn, but I don't blame him. His son's here. He's just trying to find him."

"Those men kidnapped him?"

"Yes. More like kept him as insurance. For years."

"Insurance for what?"

I thought about what was inside that old beer can left in the shed. "Probably millions of dollars worth of diamonds."

"Oh, my heavens."

"Exactly."

I knew what was at the end of two of these tunnels. One led to the forest, and the other to the waterfall. But several pathways branched off from the main tunnel, and I wasn't sure what those held. I figured Anatoli and the other man were planning an escape into the forest. But I wasn't sure how to get there from here. The only choice I had was to follow the blood. If Mikhail knew his way around these tunnels, then it was possible that Lev did as well.

Before we knew it, a branch opened up to our left. The blood followed it, as did the footprints in the dirt. I looked up at Ariella.

"You okay?"

She chirped.

"You're very brave too, Ariella. Thank you. Both of you."

We turned the corner, and more carefully this time, ran as quietly as possible. There were twists and turns, and a hostile could be behind any one of them. The bare bulbs above us were now dimmer, but I could still see tire tracks. I slowed down to inspect them. My companions stopped with me. Ariella took a break and landed next to me. But not too close.

Looking at the tracks, I realized that the tread patterns were all different. More than one car had traveled this way. I counted at least four sets, maybe more since they ran over each other. It made it difficult to determine the number. I wondered if Shaw had noticed the same thing.

My ears perked up. There was yelling up ahead, an argument of some sort. It echoed off the tunnel walls. I couldn't tell who it was, but I could tell that it wasn't in English. That was Russian.

CHAPTER 39

Alcove

The arguing continued, but I turned my head as I heard hushed talking coming from the opposite direction as well. It sounded like Shaw.

"Guys, stay here," I told Ariella and Mr. Plankk. Ariella flapped her wings in protest.

I turned and ran down the tunnel from where we had just come. The sound of quiet conversation bounced off the rock walls, making it difficult to discern where it came from or how far away it was until I was almost directly on top of them. There, in a small alcove, stood Shaw and Alvarez. And Dale Sharpe.

"Buck!" Shaw said, excited but reserved. They must have heard the Russians arguing as well. I brushed up against his leg. After a quick pat, he stood back up and addressed Dale quietly.

"Why are you here?" He was close to Dale, almost in his face. His voice had menace in it.

"This is the *last* place I wanna be—I was getting the hell out of here!"

"You've lied to us from the beginning." Shaw put his finger into Dale's chest, backing him up against the rock wall. "Give me one reason to trust you now."

"My dealership! It's gone! Haven't you seen it? There's nothing left! Except for a few cars on the lot with bullet holes!"

"Keep it down. Who are these guys?"

Dale sighed. "They came to me…"

"Who?"

"Anatoli. Some other muscle. They came to me and offered to buy out the dealership."

"And this was when?"

"I told you. About three years ago."

"Go on."

"You saw *The Godfather*, right? The whole 'I'm gonna make him an offer he can't refuse' thing? That's what they did. Made sure my name was still on everything so everyone thought it was business as usual. I sold it to them for a huge loss. But I couldn't refuse it. They made that… very clear. They knew where my mom lived. My sister. Okay? So there's nowhere for me to go. Can't go to the cops. Can't even take what little I have left and run. So now, I'm just an employee. They brought their own guys in, mechanics and managers, had to let go of just about everybody who used to work for me. And they brought this kid, you know, Mikhail. I didn't know who he was at first, but they all kept a good eye on him like he was gonna run at any moment. Toward the end, they kept him chained up. Sick, these guys."

"Lev's son."

"Right."

"Where is he now?"

"Mikhail? How am I supposed to know?"

The muffled echo of a gunshot rang out. Alvarez peeked out from the alcove, looking in the direction of where I'd left Ariella and Mr. Plankk.

"Come on," he said, "we're out of time."

CHAPTER 40

Den of Thieves

Alvarez kept a hand on the back collar of Dale's jacket and pushed him forward.

"Guys, please. Just let me leave. I'm… I haven't done anything. I'm the victim here!"

"Shut up," said Alvarez, one hand on Dale's collar, the other on the Glock he picked up in the showroom. Shaw led the way, carefully looking around curves before he continued forward. I kept pace alongside them.

We walked for a while, and I was surprised that we hadn't come across Mr. Plankk and Ariella. We'd already walked past where I'd left them. I began to worry.

More arguing up ahead. Nothing that I could decipher. But now it was much closer. Even if I couldn't understand it, the voices were becoming clearer.

The path was still wide but turned somewhat sharply up ahead. Shaw and I stepped up to the rock and glanced forward. Ahead of us was a massive opening, what looked to be as big as a football field. Shaw instantly darted back behind the rock wall, and I pushed myself flat to the ground, ears back.

It was a huge open cavern, brightly lit and filled with vehicles of every shape, size, and color. Some were covered, most were not. Golden light shot out from behind rocks high in the cavern ceiling, twenty feet above, making every car shine. They were all beautiful cars, some probably worth hundreds of thousands of dollars. Vintage Cadillacs. Chevys with massive tail fins. A cream-colored Thunderbird convertible, which looked more like a boat, with a red leather interior. Early model Mustangs. There was a late '60s Shelby. An early-century black Bugatti Royale gleamed in the light from above. I couldn't believe my eyes, but there was a deep forest green Tucker '48 Torpedo. It was like my encyclopedia of cars had come to life — every one more elegant than the last. This must be the 'hangar' of priceless automobiles that was rumoured about in town.

And right there in the front was the '58 Cadillac Coupe DeVille. It was the only car that was dirty, wheel wells brown and dripping onto the cavern floor. The bottom half of the car was coated in grime with film left from dirty snow. The back door was open.

I still couldn't see who was speaking. I crept closer.

As I moved closer, the full view of the chamber opened up to me. This other half of the cavern was filled with new model Lexus's, massive SUVs like Hummers and Navigators and Range Rovers. There was a yellow Lamborghini that looked like it had just come off the showroom floor, with a dozen more stunning cars like it. And ten feet in front of me stood Lev, pointing a Russian rifle at Anatoli, who was wearing a vest and holding a handgun to Mikhail's head. He stood next to the DeVille. The last man in Anatoli's crew stood behind the car and had his AK pointed in Lev's direction. Our direction.

They must have been trying to escape with Mikhail when Lev caught them.

More shouting, this time from Lev. Even though his son was being held at gunpoint, he refused to drop his weapon. I heard shuffling behind me and looked back.

"No, no, no, no, no!" Dale lunged forward, escaping Alvarez's grip. He moved out into the open, hands up in the air. "Please! Just... no more shooting!"

Shaw sighed heavily and leaned back against the tunnel wall, out of sight. He looked at Jay, who tilted his head up and closed his eyes. Dale walked into the chamber, leaving Shaw and Alvarez in the shadows.

"Guys, we can work this out," Dale pleaded. "Look. Just step away from the vehicles."

Anatoli's face got red. "You foolish, simple man!" He waved his gun. "Leave! Now!"

"No! These are my cars!"

"Half! Half are yours! Half are mine!" Anatoli pointed the weapon at Dale, then rethought his position and put the gun to Mikhail's head again. "I warn you to stop!"

Shaw and Alvarez exchanged looks. What was the right move here?

"Okay. Okay. Look. I'm not moving. I'm just saying... these cars are worth a fortune, you know that. They can make you a lot of money, Toli. There's nothing left. Nothing but this."

"This man, this *dibil*, he stole!" yelled Anatoli, staring at Lev. "From mob, he steals! Who do you think you are?" Anatoli pushed the barrel against Mikhail's skull.

"Toli, I run, yes," said Lev, weapon trained on Anatoli and not wavering an inch. "You, your men, in our homeland, you take my girlfriend. Even before meeting, you take her."

"Collateral."

"I go to apartment before meeting, see things torn apart. Blood. As she pack to leave you take her. I was young. Scared."

Anatoli scoffed. "Which was why you never deserved to move up. You were a child."

I looked back at Shaw and Alvarez. Jay began to move forward, but Shaw held him back, shaking his head. Not yet.

"Then you text me pic of her. You kill her," said Lev, the strength leaving his voice. "I think to myself, I'm next. So I take son and run."

"And the diamonds, Lev. If you left them, we wouldn't have followed. We would have been even. But you took them."

Lev laughed. "You think Balkanskiy would give you new territory? *Tupoy*. Dumb. I am not *tupoy*. So I run. With baby Mikhail."

Mikhail moved on the ground, adjusting his legs as he knelt. His head was still bleeding. But Lev wasn't done.

"There is no peace now," Lev said. "Because you take her. Kill her."

"You knew the rules. She is dead, and it is your fault."

"Not my fault! She wasn't part of it! He wasn't part of it!"

Dale stepped forward, hands up. "Lev, put the gun down."

Lev ignored him. "We run. Me and Mikhail. From Magadan to Alaska to the North of Dakota to here, you find us and take him. My son! You take *all* from me."

Shaw and Alvarez whispered to each other, figuring out their best move. I didn't think there *was* one.

"Not everything," said Anatoli.

"I track you to nightclub. I track my son to nightclub. But you set me up, you make it like I fire weapon into crowd and I go to jail. I sit there. For years, Anatoli, years, and every day I say to myself, I will find my son. And then kill you. And then it is okay." Lev started to falter a bit but instantly brought the barrel of the weapon back up. He was losing blood fast.

"Tell me where the diamonds are," demanded Anatoli.

Lev chuckled again, but there was no energy in it. He was dying. "They're here."

Did Lev somehow get the diamonds before he rang the doorbell at the Shaws, maybe hiding them in the Suburban? I would have heard the shed door open unless the panic at losing power covered the sound. Were they taken before then? Or was Lev lying?

"Where? Tell me. Now!" Anatoli pressed the end of the Glock into Mikhail's head.

I looked behind me as Shaw nodded. They both quickly stepped out into the light, weapons held at arm's length and unwavering. It was an uneven stalemate — our three weapons against Anatoli and his last man, the Russian standing behind the DeVille. Dale had his hands in the air, looking back and forth from Toli to the man behind the car. Shaw stepped forward, the AK-12 pointed at Anatoli's chest from 20 feet away.

"Let the boy go," he said.

"No! You drop your weapons! All of you!" Anatoli pushed the Glock against Mikhail's skull harder. "Now!"

Stand-offs were never an ideal situation. Just one itchy finger could mean death for everyone involved. If Anatoli shot Lev, Anatoli would be taken out by Shaw and Alvarez, who would then be taken out by Toli's man. If Shaw, Alvarez, or Lev shot Anatoli, the risk was too great that Toli would empty a round into Mikhail's skull. I remember reading in my Illustrated Directory of Modern Weapons that the standard trigger pull weight for a Glock was around 6 pounds. Anatoli already had closed a quarter of that distance with his trigger finger. He was ready to fire.

Mikhail trembled now, eyes wide. He looked at his father, then set his mouth in a straight line and looked down, hands behind his back.

"You give me son. I give you diamonds," said Lev.

Anatoli swung the Glock behind Mikhail's head just an inch or two and fired. Mikhail cried out. The ear-splitting crack of the gun made me shrink to the ground and flatten my ears. I can't imagine how loud the shot was for Mikhail. A tear dropped from his eye, and Toli instantly brought the gun back to the center of Mikhail's head.

"Now!" he demanded, face red and full of anger.

"Hey, hey... fine," said Shaw, pointing his AK into the air. Alvarez followed with his handgun. Lev looked back at them, a look of resignation on his face. He turned and spat in Toli's direction as he listened to his son's muted whimpers.

"I kill you," he said, throwing the automatic weapon onto the dirt in front of Anatoli. Shaw and Alvarez followed, tossing their weapons several feet forward to slide in front of Anatoli.

"Diamonds. Where are they?"

Lev tipped his chin forward. "Car. Cadillac."

CHAPTER 41

Improvisation

Anatoli waved the gun at Lev. "Show me."

Lev kept an eye on Mikhail, who was looking toward his father for some sort of guidance.

"I am sorry, son. This is over soon."

Mikhail nodded.

Lev moved forward as Toli's crewman kept his AK trained on him. Toli reached for the driver's door handle, keeping his weapon pointed at Lev, who was now approaching the vehicle with his hands in the air.

"No. Wait. Tell me," Toli said.

Lev stopped in his tracks. "In front box for gloves. In paper bag." Lev had closed half the distance between himself and his son. Now I could see that Lev had a handgun hidden in the back of his pants. This either gave us all a fighting chance or meant things would not end well. Shaw and Alvarez could see it, too.

If I could somehow distract Toli's man behind the DeVille, we'd only have one weapon to contend with—Anatoli's. I was going to have to improvise. Without a plan, I kept to the shadows and hugged the wall, carefully making my way around to the far side of the cavern to sneak back up on the other side of the DeVille.

Anatoli lowered the gun back down to Mikhail's head and said, "Dale Sharpe. Make yourself useful. Go check the glovebox."

"Me?" Dale asked.

"You. Go."

I glanced under the cars as I trotted along. Anatoli nodded his head toward the passenger door of the DeVille as Dale approached the vehicle. Dale opened the door and ducked his head inside.

Both Toli and his man's attention were diverted to the inside of the old Cadillac, craning their necks to see. Shaw and Alvarez dared to take half a step closer. I slowed down as I rounded the cavern, coming up near the other side of the DeVille, a plan forming in my mind.

I had to move closer if I wanted to pounce on Anatoli with a strong attack and sink my teeth into him. So I moved out of the shadows and padded forward, away from the safety of the cavern wall.

"Well?" Anatoli impatiently looked back at Dale inside the car.

This was it. Time to make my move. I crouched down low, ready to spring forward.

As I was making my jump calculations, a sudden yellow blur at Toli's head distracted me. Ariella! She beat her wings about him, scratching at his face with her claws. I hadn't even heard her swoop down. He batted at the air, yelling, firing his weapon into the ceiling. The sound was deafening. Rocks fell from above.

Then, a loud hiss from the opening of the cavern followed by a long trail of smoke, which ended in an orange ball of fire against the opposite wall. The earth shook. I quickly turned my head, eyes wide open.

Special Agent Valerie Hayes, her blonde hair streaked with dirt and parts of her white jacket smoldering, stood there with an RPG launcher over her shoulder, exhaust drifting out of its barrel.

Every one of my five senses was overwhelmed. The thump of the explosion, the metal twisting, the yelling — everything was lit up orange, and my body flamed with heat as the smell and taste of cordite and copper filled my mouth. Across the cavern, cars were lifted into the air as they rolled and caught fire. Anatoli stumbled and lost his weapon, allowing Mikhail to scramble away, hands scraping the ground to put some distance between them.

Lev fell to the ground as well, reaching behind his back for the handgun. He pulled it out and fired as he lay flat in the dirt, the .45 caliber bullet tearing into the back of Anatoli's kneecap. Toli screamed and dropped against the car, crawling along the ground, trying to get to the open back door. His Glock was underneath the car, unretrievable.

Toli's man fired at full auto, shooting at everything and nothing. Lev had already taken cover on the ground in front of the car. There was another explosion as a gas tank ignited. The Russian gunman hit the ground.

Lights blew out as they were hit by bullets or falling rock, sparking.

Shaw and Alvarez dove for their weapons in front of the DeVille, then rolled to safety behind other cars. Toli's man stood up and sprayed the cavern. With no real plan to rely on, I was suddenly unprotected in the middle of the chaos. I sought cover through the open rear door of the DeVille, jumping over the reaching arms of

Anatoli. I hurried under the front seat, my familiar hiding place. Flames from burning cars illuminated the inside of the old Cadillac.

More gunfire filled the chamber. Alvarez had managed to get to his weapon first and fired back at the Russian with the AK.

Dale's whole body was crammed into the passenger wheel well. He reached for the open door, slammed it closed, and hunkered down again. We made eye contact. He looked at me, confused.

Toli climbed through the back door from the ground and clawed his way in, cursing in Russian. He threw himself into the backseat, left kneecap shattered and trailing blood.

Lev ducked and ran around to the driver's side, opening the door, bullets whizzing over his head. As soon as he slid in, he slammed his door closed, turned, and brought his gun up over the seat. "You stay," he shouted. He shot once into Toli's other knee. Anatoli screamed in pain.

"Now we go for ride." Lev started the car, keys swinging from the ignition.

My ears were ringing badly. And there was no escape, the doors were closed. There was no way around it. I was going for a ride, too.

Cars were exploding all around us, we had to leave. Now. I'd hoped that Mikhail and all my people were already on their way out — soon, this place would be an apocalyptic oven.

"Wait, wait — I don't belong here." Dale tried to turn around in the small space to reach for the door handle.

But the windshield exploded in a crash of glass and chrome, and Dale shrunk back. Someone must have shot through the glass to reach the Russian behind the car. The automatic fire stopped, echoes ringing throughout the cavern in unison with the smooth rumble of the old V8 engine. Lev pumped the gas once, twice, and then we were off, plowing through the wreckage toward the rocky opening of the chamber.

CHAPTER 42

Death Wish

It felt as though we were running over rocks and car parts, and I could only hope that Shaw and Alvarez had rolled out of the way. Mikhail was off to the side somewhere, and I didn't think Lev would run over his own son. I was sure he had planned his escape route before he ever got behind the wheel. The branch that led to the forest was close to where we were now.

Anatoli was screaming in Russian from the back, trying to hold on to the side as his legs gave him no purchase. Lev maneuvered the car through the narrow cavern entrance; he risked a look backward. "I learn this word — terror. That is what is in your eyes, Toli. Terror."

"You're crazy!" Dale yelled from the floorboard. He struggled to get up as the car bounced back and forth but eventually slid into the front seat. "Lev! Let me out!" Dale tried to grab the wheel, but Lev easily pushed his hands away.

"Nyet. My friend and I have businesses to finish."

Lev stepped on the gas pedal, and the old car shot through the tunnel at almost 40 mph — it felt like 80.

"Who? Toli?" Said Dale, his voice cracking. "I'm not part of that! Let me out!"

We must have come to a split in the passage as Lev veered hard to the left. The car swayed softly, and the shocks made it feel like we were riding on water. As we passed another one of the tunnel's branches, Lev laughed and pointed to something high on the wall.

"T. For tunnel. Very good. In Armenian, yes?" This was obviously meant for Toli, who didn't answer. Lev turned to the back seat. "Yes?" He pointed the barrel of the gun at Anatoli's head.

Toli grunted and nodded, both hands covering one of his shattered kneecaps.

The pigtails. They were the Armenian letter 'T'.

We'd also just passed the only exit left before the end of the tunnel. And the waterfall.

The entire theft scheme became crystal clear now. When a vehicle was stolen, the driver would take the merchandise down the long forest road until he saw the pigtail symbol carved into a tree. Then, he follows the symbols right to the opening of the cave. The driver drops the car off in the vehicle den, exits the cavern through the tunnels, and back up into the dealership, completely unnoticed. It's the perfect way to stock the underground cavern full of stolen vehicles, alongside Dale's personal collection, without anyone ever seeing. The stolen cars are then transported to the coast in a covered car carrier, ready to be packed into the waiting cargo container. Toli and company are 200 to 400 thousand dollars richer with each shipment.

The speed of the vehicle increased. I poked my head out from under the front seat. Lev had something resembling a smile on his face.

Dale held onto the dash in front of him. "Lev! Stop the car, this is your fight, not mine!"

Lev used his chin to indicate the only exit. The front windshield.

"Oh. No. No, no, Lev, no, just stop and let me out…"

But the growl of the engine got louder, and the walls were closing in.

Toli moaned in pain from the back seat.

The passenger side of the DeVille careened into the rock wall, scraping off the side mirror in a shower of sparks. The metal around the side window crumpled and bent inwards, cracking the glass with a sharp ping. A hunk of twisted metal landed on the floorboard in front of me, spinning.

"Lev! Please!"

There was barely room for the car to fit between the tunnel walls now, but Lev kept his foot on the gas. Metal ripped and tore itself from the sides of the car in short-lived bursts of spark and flame.

"You want out, you jump." Lev pointed to the gaping hole that used to be the windshield.

I looked behind me. There were a few bullet holes with jagged glass edges in the back windshield, courtesy of Jay Alvarez, but nothing I was going to fit through. I turned back to the front and was met by two beady eyes staring straight into mine.

"Umm, hi," said Mr. Plankk, his little teeth chattering.

"What — what are you doing here?" I couldn't believe he was also here in this doomed car.

"I had to hide somewhere! How do we get out?" He was biting his two paws. He seemed to be overwhelmed.

"Right. Okay. Listen, do you trust me?"

He nodded his head.

Dale was grabbing the chome edge of where the windshield used to be.

"Mr. Sharpe!" yelled Lev. Dale looked back at him, awkwardly, one foot up on the dashboard. "Mikhail. Tell him I love him."

Dale nodded and began climbing out of the front, with one foot now on the hood. His shoe slipped. He fell against the dash but got up and tried a second time, his bloodied hand grabbing the mangled chrome.

Above the sound of the DeVille's smooth and thunderous V8 was another rumble, this one deeper. And it was getting closer.

I picked up Mr. Plankk in my mouth, trying to hold him as loosely as possible. I peeked out again, this time jumping up onto the front seat. Lev looked over at me with surprise.

"Kot! *Snova!*" yelled Lev.

Toli laughed from the back seat. "A cat. In the last moments of life, you see things, Lev. It's okay. We play as the cat and the mouse, yes?" He tried to pull himself up from his slouched position, but the pain was too great. Toli moaned and fell against the seat. "I am the cat, Lev. You are just the little mouse that runs and runs…"

Lev took one hand off the wheel and grabbed for his pistol, his anger getting the better of him. But the car hit a jagged rock, smashing the driver's side window and making Lev lose his grip on the Glock. The gun flipped end over end, through the open windshield and onto the hood of the car. It slipped off the edge and disappeared. Lev huffed and growled and tried to turn in his seat, causing his foot to press on the accelerator even harder. The car leapt forward, smashing its way through the tunnel like a pinball.

I held Mr. Plankk in my mouth and jumped to the top of the dash, humid air blasting toward us at 50mph. Dale's legs faltered underneath him as he tried to stand and climb onto the roof. He got a knee up onto the top of the cab, then his other foot followed. I jumped onto the hood.

It was covered with glass, bouncing up and down as the car was hit on both sides by rock walls. Lev pushed the car faster, harder, destroying it. Both men yelled at each other in explosive Russian words.

I looked out the back windshield, and Dale had jumped from the roof. He landed in an awkward pile on the ground, still rolling.

I looked forward. The jagged circle at the end of the tunnel was coming up fast, a hundred yards away or less, and the torrid rush of icy green water filled my ears. We had seconds left.

I timed my jump onto the roof, but as Mr. Plankk and I vaulted upwards, the car hit a wall again and was knocked around. We landed on the roof but skittered to the edge as my claws tried to dig into the metal. We were sliding off the side. I used my back paws to push us forward, but inertia was not in our favor — we were being pulled down into the meat grinder of the rock wall and the tangled metal of the car.

All I could think was that I'd never have coffee with Tabitha under the snack machine again.

With one last attempt, I kicked my back paws upward and, for just a brief moment, made contact with the rock. I kicked hard off the rock wall, pushing us out over the roof and over the trunk of the car as the DeVille sped beneath us. We landed in the dirt in a spin, eventually rolling to a stop with Mr. Plankk tucked into my chest. Once I knew we were safe, I dropped him and jumped to my feet, shaking my head to clear out the dust and glass.

The back end of the DeVille was just disappearing into the water, its tires now spinning uselessly in the air, the whole vehicle starting to tilt downward, just like in my dream. In the echos that bounced around the tunnel, I heard one of the men screaming.

The other was laughing.

The tail fins were the last to recede into the rushing water until nothing was left but the small, almost insignificant splash that came seconds later.

CHAPTER 43

A Long Walk

"Oh, my gracious." Mr. Plankk shivered on the dirt floor as we watched the rush of water fall over the tunnel's opening. It was almost as if the car had never been there. He looked up at me.

"Thank you for saving me, Mr. Buckleberry. I thought —"

"I know. Me too."

We turned our backs to the waterfall and began to walk in the opposite direction.

"Did we get the bad guys, Mr. Buckleberry?" He had to double his pace to keep up with my saunter.

I looked down at him as we walked. "Yes, I think we did."

"Were there really diamonds in the glovebox? Did you see?"

"I don't know. Mr. Sharpe was trying to open it, but it must have been locked." I didn't tell him that the last place I saw the diamonds was just above my office.

"How much do you think they're worth?"

What I had seen in the old beer can was something beyond my imagination. Some of the stones seemed to be rough, others polished and cut. All of them must have been held together with a type of glue, something water-soluble. This probably made it easier for Lev to carry without worrying about them escaping from the hole in the top or making noise. If he needed one, he'd cut one out from the glue carefully with a knife. The value of hundreds of diamonds like that was unfathomable. I figured at least 100 million. Maybe five times that. I had no way to tell.

"Lots," I told him.

We rounded a curve and came upon a man walking slowly, hugging the wall to the right. It was Dale. He must have sprained an ankle when he jumped off the top of the speeding DeVille. He turned his head backward as he heard us approaching.

"Well, look who it is. Super Kitty."

I said the only thing I could. "Meow."

"You know, you displayed some pretty brave heroics back there. What were you doing — wait a minute, you have a pet mouse?"

He turned around and bent down to scratch my head. Mr. Plankk was less than pleased with being referred to as a mouse and even less trusting. He kept behind me.

"I thought cats and mice were enemies."

"I'm a vole," said Plankk, but all Dale heard was some squeaks.

The way back through the tunnels was long, but we eventually met up with Shaw, Alvarez, and Agent Hayes jogging toward us from the opposite direction.

"Buck!" Shaw yelled, and I jumped up into his arms. "I thought we'd lost you," he said, and I nudged the top of my head under his chin. He smiled and scratched behind my ear.

"Wait," said Valerie, "this is your cat from home?"

Shaw chuckled. "It is. He likes to follow trouble. Don't you, buddy?"

I gave a short meow.

"Come on, we can't stop now." Shaw started jogging with me. "This tunnel has to end somewhere."

We ran into Dale, slowly walking out of the shadows toward us. "Don't bother," he said. "They're not coming back."

"Dale, you okay?" asked Alvarez.

It took him a few seconds to answer. "Nope. Not alright." He sagged against the tunnel wall. "Not my best day."

Alvarez went to check him out and bent down next to him.

Where was Mikhail? Did he make it out of the chamber after Agent Hayes fired the RPG?

"You need to get him a vest," said Agent Hayes, pointing to me as I blinked slowly at her. "Tactical. They sell them, you know."

Shaw considered. "That," he said, "is not a bad idea." He adjusted me in his arms, and I put both paws on his shoulders. I watched Mr. Plankk keeping pace just a few feet behind. He seemed upset that his little legs had to take him right back from where we had just come.

"Dale," said Alvarez, "you need a shoulder to lean on? Looks like you twisted your ankle."

"No. I need a shoulder to cry on." He looked straight at Valerie.

"We needed a diversion, Mr. Sharpe. Several lives were in danger. I'm sorry about your cars."

"A few well-placed gunshots might have had the same effect, you know. Just saying."

"I didn't think the only weapon I'd find would be a Soviet grenade launcher. But there you go. How did you get out?"

Dale looked at Shaw. "Your cat and I jumped through the windshield and over the back of the car."

"That's it, Buck, you're getting the vest," said Shaw. "Maybe a bulletproof one. I understand you want to be an outdoor cat, but come on."

He was right. In the past 24 hours, I'd been in situations where most humans never found themselves. But I guess this was just my line of work now. Though I seriously doubted they made bulletproof vests for cats.

"What happened to Lev and Anatoli?" Shaw asked.

Dale just pointed toward the back end of the tunnel. "See for yourself. It's not far. I'll wait here."

Shaw, Alvarez, and Valerie weren't in the worst of moods, which probably meant that Mikhail was okay. They must have left him somewhere safe instead of making him walk the miles of tunnels. I hoped he was okay.

We continued to walk toward the end of the tunnel. Shaw and company had no idea what had happened to the car, and I'm not even sure they knew there was a waterfall at the end. But we heard it soon enough. And as we got closer, we felt it. Not only the rumble in our chests but the humidity in the air, the breeze from outside blowing the vaporized water droplets against my fur. Or, in their case, against their skin.

Shaw and Alvarez looked at each other. Jay spoke up.

"We're in the old Ore Knob copper mine. That's the drop in the river up ahead." He pointed.

In another two minutes, we were there. The cold and dampness seeped into our skin, and I jumped down from Shaw's grasp.

The water fell in a torrent, with chunks of ice dropping out of nowhere into the icy pool a hundred and forty-some feet below. The entire edge of the outcropping was covered in rime, and we had to watch our footing. It was very slick.

Valerie found the heavy-duty zip-tie packages first, set off to the side between two car parts I couldn't identify. She stuck her hand a few inches back into her jacket sleeve and picked up one of the packages with the edge of her cuff.

"Look. Restraints?" she asked Shaw and Alvarez. She placed them inside her jacket pocket.

Alvarez kicked at the rusted flywheels and motor parts. "Or, they used a few of them together to attach these things to the body. Weigh it down. Then toss it over."

The three of them looked over the edge. Thousands of gallons of water fell past us and dropped into the grey-green pool below. Nothing would survive that fall. And nobody would break free from a hundred pounds of metal strapped to them submerged in a pool that was probably deeper than the Shaw's house. This was a death stage. The last stop for those who decided to go against the mob, or threatened to leave, or had come too close to the truth. Like Alec Popov.

The trio said nothing, then turned back the way they came.

CHAPTER 44

Ruins

We reached Dale on the way back, and he shuffled along with us in silence. The walk took what seemed like forever.

Shaw spoke up. "Jay. You feel like a jog? I'm worried about Mikhail. I know we left him in a safe spot, but he wasn't in great condition to begin with."

"That's what I was thinking. See you soon," he said and took off down the tunnel.

We were all worn out, and this long walk sapped the last of our strength. After a minute or so, Shaw spoke up and said to Dale, "Tell me about Lev."

Dale sighed. "So I get a letter about six months ago. On the driver's floorboard of my XT4. Says he's Mikhail's dad. Horrible writing. Horrible English. Like, I thought it was a prank at first. But this guy, he knew stuff. So… I realized that it was for real. Told me that he used to work for the mob in Russia a long time ago and that the guys who ran the dealership now were some bad 'persons' he said, from Armenia. Like I didn't know that already. And that he'd run off with some jewels or something when he was younger, and he's been on the run with his son ever since. But these guys, they find the kid and they take him, right? It took some time, but eventually, Lev tracks him here. Knew he was working here. Well, not working. But you know what I mean."

"They've kept Mikhail for three years?" asked Shaw, incredulous.

"Something like that. When he got here, he was like 15." That must have been just before Lev tracked Toli and his group to Raleigh. They take Mikhail sometime before the nightclub incident, weeks or days before. Lev tracks them down but gets arrested trying to rescue his son. He has to wait more than three years before he can start searching for Mikhail again.

"How did you keep in touch?" Shaw asked. "With them watching?"

"You want the whole story?"

"We've got the time."

"Okay. So… my mom died. God rest her soul."

"Sorry about your mom."

"Yeah, thanks. So, she dies, and of course, I go down to Florida for the funeral. And they send somebody with me, right, just like they did with Bernie Baer. Is he okay by the way?"

"Yes. Keep talking."

"Fine. So, in this letter, Lev gives me his cell number. On my phone, I have a list of all my inventory with VINs and things, and I hide his number in the VIN for a fake car. Just in case they look at my phone, which they do. But they never put it together. How could they, right? So, this guy, Yaroslav—we call him Yari—he and I are rooming together at a hotel in Tampa for my mom's service. And the second night I'm there, I tell him I need to go down to the business center to, you know, take care of business. He says he'll come with me. Fine. So I go down to the center, sit in front of a computer, and pull up some legal documents for car purchases and inventory and stuff, and I print them out. I write on them, adding notes and comments and things, and Yari watches me doing this for a bit, looks at what I printed out, and then goes and sits in a chair on the other side of the desk. I take a blank sheet of paper and write a note for Lev. Put it in the middle of all the other papers. The hotel has Fax Over Internet Protocol, not to bore you. But I send the fax to Lev's phone."

"Smart."

"You know how long faxes take to go through? That was the longest 10 minutes of my life. So once it goes through, I put the papers through the shredder and tell Yari that maybe the bar's open, and we both have a few drinks. Hate to say it, but he wasn't bad company."

"What did your note say?"

"Okay. So, I hadn't done spots up until last year. I mean, like, as talent."

"Spots?"

"Commercials. So I told Lev that if I ever advertised a 2020 CT5, that was the code. That it was probably the best time to come get his son. I mean, with a crew of men armed with all kinds of stuff, there really is no best time. But there had been a lot of infighting, and tensions were running high."

"What if he didn't see it? The commercial?"

"No, no, all our spots go up on YouTube. I told him all he has to do is check our channel once a day."

"Alright. So Lev sees you're selling a 2020 CT5."

"Exactly."

"And he comes for his son."

"Right."

Shaw looked over at Val. "You think that's what the attempted murder incident up in Kelso was all about? The timing adds up. Maybe the guy he was after up there knew something, maybe Lev had no intention of killing him. Just... getting some information out of him."

"Maybe," said Val. "He's out of prison for a few months, always checking the YouTube feed, probably living somewhere in NC, then when he sees the 2020 CT5 on sale, he comes to town."

"That's what happened," said Dale. "And Mikhail, he's a good kid, he hadn't seen his dad in, what, like three or four years. So... I kinda... brokered a deal. By fax."

Shaw and Val looked at each other. "A deal?" she asked.

"To see his son. They kept him in a locked room when he wasn't working, but I knew where the key was. So I told him I could arrange a meeting with his son. For a jewel. He said he had jewels. It was a diamond, with like... dried brown Elmer's glue all over it."

"That doesn't make any sense," said Val. "Glue?"

"I don't know what to tell you. That's what it was."

"Look at it this way," said Shaw. "Lev's young, a kid, really. Has all these diamonds. Then his girlfriend is taken and killed, and he realizes he's got to escape with his son. But what do you do with the diamonds? You can't just put them in a paper bag and hop on a fishing trawler. He put them in that old beer can and filled it with glue so that they didn't rattle around or fall out, and now he can easily toss it in his backpack or whatever. When he needs one, he digs one out with his penknife."

That's exactly what I'd thought.

"Oh," said Dale.

"Why not just take his son then? And escape?" Val asked. "At the meeting you set up?"

"He wanted revenge. He wanted them dead. A surprise attack. If all of a sudden Mikhail goes missing, everyone's on high alert."

"Okay," she said. "How did Lev get to the meeting with his son?"

"Oh, I gave Lev one of my cars. Well, sold it to him."

The DeVille.

"Dropped it off for him at Courtland County Park. Nobody's there in the winter."

"So he walked there to get the car? Where was he staying?"

"I don't know. He said he was going to find a motel or something."

That's it. That's why I first saw him in the DeVille, cruising past our room at the Highlander Motel. He wasn't looking for Shaw. He was looking for a place to stay, but once he saw the State Trooper sitting out front, he knew he couldn't stay there.

"Wait. Two hours ago, Lev showed up on my doorstep. In the middle of a snowstorm. Why? How did he get there? There's no way he walked in this storm. And I didn't see a car."

Dale looked sheepishly at the ground. "I went with him. He said he needed to visit your house. He wouldn't tell me why. I made him promise that he wasn't going to kill you. Or, you know, your family."

"Wow, thanks, Dale. You're a real stand-up guy," said Shaw.

"I told him the only way he was going was if I went with him, to make sure."

"Right. Because you would have stopped him from killing me and my family."

"I knew he wasn't going to. He talked about you. He thought he could trust you."

"So what, you drove him to my house? And just dropped him off in the middle of a storm?"

"He drove. It was his car — he paid for it. He parked on Oakridge, a street over from you. But I could see. I saw you put him to his knees, and someone pointed a shotgun at his head. I panicked. So I took the car and came back here."

Did Lev go to the shed, get the diamonds, then turn himself into Shaw? No. Shaw patted him down. He would have found the beer can.

"Came back where? You were here during all this gunfire?" Shaw asked.

"Hell, no. I parked the car in the cavern. Then I hoofed it, I could hear Toli coming. You guys ran into me as I was trying to leave."

"So you took the car you had just sold to Lev."

"Look. I didn't expect him to ring your doorbell."

"What *did* you expect?"

Eventually, the air darkened with the smoke from the burning vehicles, and the acrid scent of fuel and burning material hit our noses. We'd reached the vehicle cavern.

I wanted to see inside, to go down that shaft and see what was left of the burning cars, if anything. But the smoke was too thick, and there was no way we were going to head down that passageway with anything but firefighters' equipment.

Shaw put me in his jacket, and the others held their arms over their faces. We could hear the fire eating away at everything inside the chamber — it roiled and flashed and consumed leather seats, foam, fiberglass, rubber fuel lines, rubber tires. There was not much that would escape its wrath. Maybe in a few days, the cavern could be explored to see what was left. But not now.

It seemed like the majority of the fumes were being sucked out to the forest, and once we passed that branch, the air started to clear up. Shaw put me back on his shoulder, and I saw Mr. Plankk keeping pace with us. He was low enough to the ground that the smoke had little effect on him. He waved at me while he ran, and I lifted my paw to acknowledge him.

We rounded a corner, and there was Mikhail slumped against the rock wall, dirty and bruised. Alvarez crouched next to him, hand on his shoulder. He must have told him the news about his father — Mikhail had his hand to his face.

We gathered together, walking the rest of the way. The pace was slow, but in ten minutes, we reached the bottom of the stairwell to the dealership above. One glance up the stairs, and we knew we'd have to find another way. Flames licked and roared at the top of the stairwell, peeling the paint and blackening the walls. A rush of the cold outside air hit us as the fire sucked in oxygen from the closest shaft — the one that led to the service bays.

Mikhail pointed to the left.

We made our way up the dirt ramp, which ended at the large green door, the door where every stolen car had been driven through and loaded onto the cargo carrier. Those days were now over.

Shaw pushed the door open a little further to make it easier for Alvarez and Mikhail to fit through. Once the door was open, the scene before us looked nothing like what we saw earlier.

The roof was gone or hanging down into the bay itself. Snow fell into the entire service area. Steel beams stretched into the sky, insulation and plastic sheeting on fire at the tops of them, like burning beacons. The floor was littered in heaps of fiery piles. Every one of the cars that remained was engulfed in flames. Even Mr. Plankk's oil painting of Alec Popov danced in a glow of sparks and fire. The rolling garage door was now outside in the snow, still on fire in places. The plastic snapped and crinkled in glowing patterns as it burned.

I looked for Ariella in the wreckage or flying above. There were no signs of her or Hamilton Waters.

We carefully made our way through the conflagration, stepping over burning chunks of rubber and roof lining. Parts of the roof fell through as we made our way out, crashing against the floor in a loud ploof and sending out sparks and licks of fire in every direction.

Once we were outside, I wiggled free from Shaw's embrace. Fire was everywhere. As we made our way around the building, I thought that was at least one good point — it wasn't nearly as cold.

The only thing untouched by the cruelty of the fire was the 22-foot Dale Sharpe Cadillac sign that stood unlit at the front of the property. Everything else was destroyed. Bare steel beams reached into the sky, no longer holding glass but framing the destruction around them. Glass littered the ground and sparkled like golden jewels, reflecting and refracting the surrounding fires. Cars were aflame, burning high into the night air, black smoke mixing with the falling snow. Even a dozen fire trucks couldn't save what was left. We stood, huddled together, watching as the building fell in upon itself, creating flames as high as the trees and heat like nothing we had ever felt.

Either the snow was being melted by the intense heat, or the storm had actually abated. There wasn't a flake in the sky.

"I see you borrowed my cruiser," said Shaw as Valerie walked up to him, undoing her jacket.

"I wasn't standing on the sidelines for this one. Your wife knew I was serious and even offered to drive, but I wouldn't let her. At least I was able to make a difference."

"At just the right time. I'm going to start calling you Schwarzenegger, shooting things up with an RPG like that." He chuckled.

"Well, I *did* come back."

"Wait a minute, how *did* you know to come here?"

"I was ten minutes behind you, Catherine and Whitney tried to talk me out of it. Had another cup of coffee and a handful of Tylenol. This place is on the way to the station, and it was already half-destroyed by the time I got here. When I saw your Suburban inside, it was go-time."

Alvarez stepped up to them. "Boss, the radio's working. Every available is on their way. Along with CSFD."

"There's no saving this place," said Shaw.

"Fire like this, they're gonna need to investigate. Wait till they get to the tunnels."

Shaw looked at both of them. "I saw a fire on the news once when I was a kid, started in a tire dump in Virginia. You know how long it took to put out?"

Neither Alvarez nor Val answered.

"Nine months. Not sure how they're going to get this under control. Maybe they'll just let it burn itself out down there. But I don't think anyone's going into those tunnels any time soon."

They all contemplated that thought for a little while before Alvarez spoke up.

"Question," he said, "anyone know where those diamonds are?"

CHAPTER 45

CSPD

The diamonds. Were they really in the glovebox, like Lev said, or was that just a distraction to set things in motion? Could the final location of the diamonds have been something Lev and his son were talking about when I was catnapped in the DeVille? That was very possible.

It had been a long day for everyone. Well, night. With the end of the storm, the FBI was finally able to send a chopper up from the Hickory office, and a team debriefed everyone involved. The fires above ground were put out by CSFD as the sun began to filter through the forest behind the ruins of Dale Sharpe Cadillac. The water from the hoses turned into pellets of ice once most of the flames had been extinguished. The fires below ground, we were told, would burn for days. Perhaps weeks. They began working on a solution as soon as what remained of the dealership had become a pile of smoldering rubble.

SAIC Peter Roman had personally made the trip up to commend Agent Hayes and lead the debriefing. He seemed like a no-nonsense kind of guy. He wore a gray business suit, and I don't think I saw him smile once. He was probably exactly the type of man who needed to lead this investigation. Hayes had several pieces of evidence in her desk at the dealership, which was now gone, of course, burned in the fire. Others she had at her small apartment in town. But back at CSPD, Shaw and Alvarez had overseas transport receipts for the stolen vehicles, as well as a stack of papers proving the massive amount of ID theft that took place at Dale Sharpe Cadillac. And Roman wanted to see all of it, which was good. Because I wanted to see Tabitha.

We rode in the back compartment of one of the fire trucks. Shaw sat by the window and held me on his lap. As we traveled back into town, I looked out the window at the mounds of snow by the side of the road and the way it made the trees glitter. Something caught my eye, and I quickly looked up to the sky.

A little yellow bird was keeping pace with the fire truck. She swooped down once, close to the window, and then was gone. Ariella was safe. I smiled.

Maybe there'd be a message from Mr. Waters when I returned to the office. The last I saw him, he was running for safety once the gunfire erupted, so I hoped he was okay.

One of the firemen had left a styrofoam cup of coffee in a holder on the door, and Shaw didn't pull me back when I put my entire head into it and lapped it up. It was the first bit of peace I'd had in quite a while.

"Well, look who it is. I thought I'd never see you again," Tabitha said as she slinked up to me in the main hallway of the station. Everyone had gathered in the conference room.

"Really?"

"No, dummy. But communications were out for a few hours. Figured you'd be able to hold your own."

"I did more than that. I practically solved the case."

"Is that so? I wonder if I helped any. Or Shaw. Maybe that pretty FBI woman."

"Fine. It wasn't all me. I'm just saying—"

"What?"

"That I, you know. Detected."

Tabitha sat in front of me and looked me straight in the eyes. "Yes. You certainly did." Her mouth curled into a smile. "And you were very brave while doing it. I've heard things."

"Like what?" I asked.

"Like, a certain cat confronted some ruthless international criminals and was even involved in a gunfight." She nudged the top of my head.

"And?"

"And then he bravely led the police to the location of their underground base of operations."

"Mm-hmm. And then?"

"And then I heard that he jumped out of a moving vehicle just before it plunged over a huge waterfall."

I put a paw on her head, effectively telling her politely to stop. She did.

"I, I think I lost a friend, Tabitha, whether he knows it or not. Lev was a good man. No matter what he was involved with before. All he wanted to do was find his son."

She sighed. "I'm sorry, Buckleberry."

"It's okay. He knew he had sins to pay for. Both he and Anatoli. So he did what he thought was best."

"What about Mikhail? And the diamonds, what happened to them?"

"Wow, you really did learn a lot while I was gone."

"Well, I overheard Roman on the phone with the U.S. Marshals. That can only mean one thing."

"Witness Protection."

"Right. So there's going to be a case brought against someone," Tabitha said, peering around the corner to see if we were still in the clear.

"I hope it's not Dale. Not that he's completely innocent, but there were a lot of circumstances beyond his control."

"They'll figure all that out. What about the diamonds?" she asked again.

"I might know a little something about that…"

Tabitha and I walked down the main hall to the block of detention cells. We didn't have to be buzzed in, the heavy door was open. There were only two people behind bars, and that was not because they were criminals, I figured, but because they were both involved in a crime. Dale and Mikhail.

A medic had cleaned up Mikhail's forehead. Hopefully, there was no concussion, but it was hard to imagine there wasn't. Dale had bandages on his hand and wrist.

They were whispering but stopped when Dale noticed me.

"How about that! There you are. Your name's Buck! Come here, kitty…" he said and bent down close to me from the other side of the bars. "You're a good cat. I'm glad you made it, buddy. When I saw you in that car, I thought I was hallucinating. What were you doing there?"

I nudged against his hand between the bars as he scratched behind my ears. He petted Tabitha as well and then turned back to Mikhail, voice low.

"So I'll say that, yes, I saw the diamonds in the glovebox. That'll be my statement. Yes, it's a lie, but no one's ever going to know. I'll say they must have fallen out into the river, gone forever. There's so many little mining places up here in the mountains, like tourist traps. They give you a bucket of dirt, and you sift through it into a trough of running water. Imagine what that'll do for the tourist industry — thousands of people coming here to pan for diamonds in the New River. It's a good thing, really, I mean, my statement. Good for the county. It'll become like a legend." He sighed. "You know where they really are. Don't tell me, I don't want to know. You take them. They're yours now. Unless, you know, you want to drop one by for me. If you feel so inclined."

CHAPTER 46

Doormat

Much later that day, Shaw left in his cruiser after most of the loose ends had been tied up. He'd let his insurance company know about the Suburban. Who knows what the coverage is on a bullet-riddled, burned-out shell of an SUV involved in stopping an international crime syndicate? Hopefully, they'd cover it.

On the way home, Shaw took me to Dr. Wells, my veterinarian. To her house, actually—nothing would be open today and possibly tomorrow. She was able to look at my paws, get all the glass out, and give them a good hydrogen peroxide bath, rinsing them with saline.

We finally pulled into our driveway. It was good to be home.

I didn't stop in my office right away but let Patrick and Frannie fawn over me for a bit, and Catherine gave me some tuna along with my dry food. I can't remember being as content as I was right then. Shaw and Catherine had been talking about Mikhail.

"Honey, the law cannot compel a person to enter Witness Protection. It's up to the individual," said Shaw.

"But, he's so young, isn't he scared? I mean, what if the Armenian mafia decided to come after him? Where is he going to go?"

"I don't know. He's smart. It's up to him. If he needs help, he has numbers he can call."

"But why wouldn't he want protection?"

"Because he wants freedom, Cath. That's all I can come up with."

There were about two feet of snow on the front porch, which Shaw needed to shovel out, so instead of waiting until morning when it froze over, he decided to do the job then. I helped him by sitting in one of the Adirondack chairs Shaw had cleared for me. I watched him shovel.

He was doing a pretty good job. When he got to the front door, the shovel cleared the welcome mat in one clean swipe. But underneath the mat, something long and yellow stuck out, suddenly uncovered. A manila envelope. He bent down to pick it up, then moved me gently aside to sit in my chair. He pulled off his gloves.

Undoing the clasp, Shaw pulled out a crudely hand-written letter. After the letter, something heavy fell out of the envelope and onto the porch. He picked it up, blew the snow off, and turned it in his hand. It was a dirty rock. No, wait. As he moved it, it sparkled in the light of the afternoon sun. I knew exactly what it was.

He palmed the rough diamond and read the letter.

Dear Mr. Shaw,

I am about to turn myself in to you. But before I do, I need you to know some things about me and Mikhail. I do not know if you will arrest me or put me in the prison but there are things I must say in case you do not give me chance. But I trust you will. First I am sorry. For attacking you after my arrest. At that moment I know that I not see my son for many years. And I become angry. And you are there so I attack you. Sorry from my heart. But now I find him and if all works out, he and I will leave and go far far away. Please help us doing this. Years ago I left Bratva the minute they kill Mikhail's mother. It stop then. Believe me in this. No longer am I part of that madness. And from that moment I do all for him. We run. We hide. I kill because I had to kill. We do this for 15 years, we move and move and hide and run but then they find Mikhail. Bratva. They know I will come for him and trade him for diamonds. It took long time, but I find Toli and my son here in Copper Summit. These are bad men that have him. So I plan and prepare. But now I know I can not do it myself and I need help. You will help me yes? If not and you take me to the prison, please you keep Mikhail safe? In exchange I give you diamond and it will help with expense. You understand that it is not meant for you, yes? Not a bribe. Is for Mikhail. There is more but I don't know if he will get it. He knows where rest of diamonds are, but he is captive. So, I leave this rock in envelope. You help me free him. I am not good man. But I am good father. Please, you help us.

There was an illegible signature at the bottom. But we knew who it was from.

And Bratva — the name the various Russian organized crime groups gave themselves. Solntsevskaya Bratva. I learned that from the INTERPOL fax.

Lev had given himself up to save his son. He knew he was going to die. And isn't that every good man's dream? To sacrifice himself for a greater good? Lev was wrong. He was a good father. And a good man.

It took me some time to paw my office door clear. It was completely covered in snow, along with the windows, but I didn't worry about those. I just wanted to get inside and steep some nipped Earl Grey. I turned the knob and pushed the door open, delicate snow drifting in.

Oh no. Mr. Tuttle. I had forgotten about him. I don't think he'd moved since I left him a day or so ago. He was still snoring and slowly spinning, so I'm sure he'd made several revolutions.

Before waking him, I went to check my email. Lifting the lid of my laptop, I saw I had a message from Hamilton Waters:

Home safe. Be in touch.

A beaver of few words, that Mr. Waters.

I walked up to the turtle in my office and nudged him.

"Mr. Tuttle."

Nothing.

I made three quick taps on his belly like a prizefighter getting in some fast right jabs. "Mr. Tuttle!"

That stirred him from his rest, and his eyes opened, slowly focusing in on me.

"Yes?"

"It's time to go. I need to clean, and the storm is over."

"You don't say?" He worked his feet in the air, almost as if testing if they would support his weight should he decide to turn over.

"Yes. Also, I believe if you build a new house, I can almost guarantee that it will not be disturbed again."

"You mean stolen."

"Yes. Fine. It won't be stolen. Now, let me help you…" I pushed against his shell, and as he groaned, I was able to give him enough leverage so that he flipped over, landing on the braided rug with a big huff.

"Thank you, Mr. Buckleberry, for letting me sleep here for a few minutes. I think I needed the rest."

"Of course. You had nowhere to go in the storm. But now, things are somewhat back to normal. So, off you go."

"Yes, yes. I shall invite you to my housewarming party once I build a new one. If you can fit in it."

"If not, I'll admire it from the outside."

"Very well, Mr. Buckleberry. Again, thank you for not only your hospitality but for ensuring that I have a safe place to build. I hope it wasn't too much trouble." I started to guide him toward the front door.

"No trouble at all, Mr. Tuttle. Now, if you don't mind…" I started, but heard a creak in the wood above. My ears perked up.

"As Samuel Johnson said, 'The true measure of a man, or cat, is how…'" But I had tuned Mr. Tuttle out completely. I scampered to the corner of my office and climbed up the bookcase to the small slit in the ceiling. I narrowed my eyes and looked into the shed.

The door was open. And there, bending down to retrieve the old beer can, was Mikhail. He shook the can and smiled.

If you've enjoyed The Cat That Chased Cadillacs, turn the page for the first chapter in B. Buckleberry's next adventure, THE CAT THAT FOLLOWED PHANTOMS, releasing in October 2024.

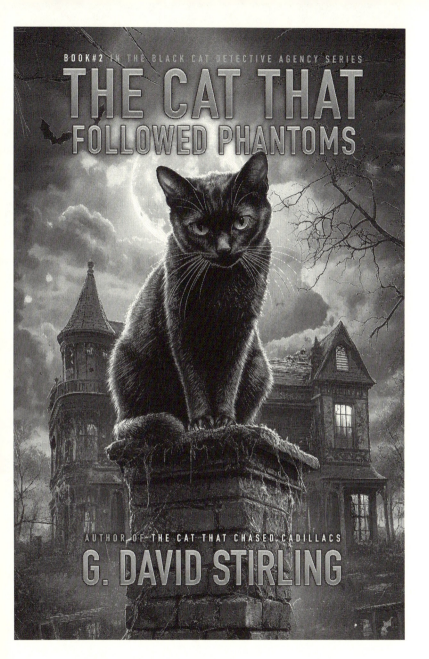

1
NIGHT VISITOR

I was up late reading an old leather-bound Edgar Allan Poe collection when the night thundered softly, and the rain started to beat against my office window — rapping, tapping. Perhaps you can guess which story I held between my paws. It's more of a poem, really. But it never failed to chill me. I could always sense my pupils widen to full circles when my eyes got to this stanza:

But the silence was unbroken, and the stillness gave no token,
And the only word there spoken was the whispered word, "Lenore?"
This I whispered, and an echo murmured back the word, "Lenore!"
Merely this and nothing more.

While on the front door of my office are the chiseled words: B. Buckleberry — Black Cat Detective Agency, even I can get a little scared from time to time.

As I sat in the dimly lit office, my large orange eyes looked up and scanned the room. I was alone, right? I closed the leather cover of the book. What if someone was right outside my door? Or my window? I put my furry face to the glass and looked out into the forest, both paws shielding my eyes from the glare.

TAP TAP TAP

I let out a shocked mewl and flinched backward, almost falling off the shelf where I was reading. There, in the dim shaft of light from my Banker's lamp was a sliver of a bird, yellow, with black eyes that reflected the amber glow of my office interior.

"Ariella!"

Gathering myself, I rolled from my back over to all four paws. I jumped down and headed to the door. As soon as I opened it, the autumn breeze ushered in a cold chill. I called out to her again and invited her indoors, but she shook her head and wouldn't move from outside the window.

"Ah. Okay," I said, realizing she was reluctant to sidle past me, a cat. As it was, I had to suppress my cat senses every time she stepped into my office. Controlling my natural feline propensities when in close proximity to a bird of any type was slowly becoming easier, but I still couldn't manage to stop my chittering from time to time. Which, of course, made Ariella hesitant to trust me. And she was looking a bit plump lately. But I stepped back into my office and sat behind my desk, giving her safe passage inside.

Her head peered around the corner of the door, ensuring that I was indeed far enough away from her that it would be safe to proceed. She placed one foot into the office.

"Ariella, it's c-c-c-c-clear. C-c-c-c-come on in…"

With a crash, more thunder boomed, and a lightning flash lit up my office in blue-white. She ran inside all the way and slammed the door.

Ariella is my messenger, in fact, the official messenger of Black Cat Detective Agency, and she knows I'm not going to hurt her. And I know I'm not going to hurt her. But our ingrained behaviors are difficult to overcome. For each of us. Usually, I'll summon her, so it's very rare that she shows up on her own. Especially asking to come inside. This must be important. There was only one problem, though. I don't speak Finch. Or Bird.

"Is everything o-k-k-kay?" I asked her. It was after 10 pm, and all the birds I knew flew back to their nests before dark. The skies had been black for over three hours.

She nodded her head up and down. Okay. She's not hurt, nor is anyone else. I think. She looked outside the windows at the rain as it started to fall heavily.

"Did someone come to you with a case?" I asked. Yes, she nodded her head up and down several times enthusiastically.

"Oh. Good. I was beginning to think I'd have to start putting ads on C-C-C-Critter." Critter is a neighborhood app that keeps all the animals informed about things we need to know; mercury levels in the river, the potential for severe weather, as well as all the obligatory gossip, of course. For instance, last week, I would never have known that several of Ranger's cows had escaped. Ranger is a well-known black and white Australian Shepherd. He's the only dog on the property, and herding and keeping an eye on over 100 heads of cattle by himself must be exhausting. But after 22 minutes on Critter, Ranger followed the posts about the cow's whereabouts and was able to track them to the parking lot of the Piggly-Wiggly on Main Street. From there, he herded them home on his own.

I asked Ariella who it was that was in need of my services.

Ariella ruffled her feathers, getting herself ready for our game of Charades. She put a wing on top of her head, closed her eyes, and pretended to snore, though it sounded more like a squeaky door opening.

"Snore? Sleep? Head? Sleepyhead! Sleepyhead Hetta!"

She jumped up and down and nodded. Hetta was a miniature pot-bellied pig that only talked about two things — her boyfriend, fellow pot-belly Richard Swinbourne, and shopping. If it wasn't one of those two subjects, Hetta could not reliably carry on a conversation. Also, as if this weren't barrier enough to becoming good acquaintances with the little pig, she had a slight narcolepsy condition. At the drop of a hat, she could fall into a deep sleep. It didn't happen all the time, but when it did, Hetta would zone out for a few seconds, nothing too long.

"Is she missing?" I asked Ariella.

She shook her head no.

"Is a friend of hers missing?"

She shook her head no.

"Is she missing something?"

Ariella jumped up and down a few times. Then, she drew a circle around her wrist with the tip of her wing.

"She's missing a bracelet."

Correct, she nodded.

"And Hetta believes it was stolen?"

Yes, yes, nodded Ariella.

"Is this bracelet valuable?"

Yes.

"So it's worth a lot of money!"

Ariella touched her bright yellow chest and drew a small heart there.

"Oh, it has sentimental value." Ariella nodded again. "Darn. I was hoping for a big stolen diamond bracelet heist that only the most cunning of thieves could pull off. And only the smartest of detectives could solve."

Ariella shrugged her shoulders.

"So, why bring this to me now? It's way past your bedtime."

Ariella made multiple gestures with her wings, lifting her feet like she was marching, drawing triangles in the air, pretending to feast on — oh my goodness, was that a turkey leg she was eating? — then bending her feathers and rippling them in front of herself as the tips moved down to the floor.

"Ah! You and Arristarkis were at the first night of Harvest Fest. It closed down for the evening because of the rain, and you're just getting back. And you ran into Sleepyhead Hetta there?"

Ariella jumped up and down, clapping the ends of her wings.

"I see. Fine. And you told Miss Hetta to come by in the morning, yes? This time is normally outside of my working hours…" Yes, she nodded. She drew a one, a zero, and the letters AM in the air. "Good," I told her. I mean, technically, I open at 9, but that's just so early.

Another small head bob, this one with intention, as her two black eyes looked straight at me.

"Of course. You've earned it." She walked to the door, opened it with her foot, and hopped outside into the rain. Coming around the edge of the desk, I grabbed a handful of wriggling worms from the silver bucket I kept on the floor. I walked to the open door and tossed them outside on the ground. "Thank you, Ariella. I hope you and your husband had a good time at the Festival. I hear they're making some great changes this year." She ignored me as she pecked and ate.

At Harvest Fest, I was sure both Ariella and Arristarkis had eaten endless scraps of funnel cake, pumpkin pie, and fried Twinkies. But outside my window, the little yellow bird continued to chirp and pounce in front of the worms I gave her, gulping them down one by one while the sky lit the clouds blue.

Harvest Fest is the town festival that runs the week before Halloween, with the last night falling on the 30th, allowing the kids to have the 31st for Trick 'r Treating. There are rides, food, games, bands, pumpkin picking, jack o'lantern and scarecrow judging, corn mazes, and a haunted house. People come from all over the state and beyond to attend. But best of all, in my opinion, is the cider from White Woods Winery. Every year, I ask my goat friend who works there for a bottle of Teacher's Pet, made with a variety of late-season local apples, aged in bourbon barrels for a year, which adds subtle notes of oak and caramel. Bumper usually comes by my office with a bottle of the stuff hooked behind his horns. But I hadn't seen him yet.

Fall was probably my favorite season, for so many reasons, not the least of which was Harvest Fest. So many new scents and new sights. And fresh gastronomical treats like pumpkin, cider, and the white tips of candy corn.

The Shaws had lined their front porch with tiny little pumpkins and gourds, so occasionally, I would jump up on the railing and pick one up in my mouth. Taking it back to my office under the shed, I'd patiently bite around the stem until I could take the top off and then scoop out the insides with my paws and eat. Admittedly, I needed to take a bath after, but with a fire in the fireplace, that was the height of luxury.

It was late. Ariella had already flown home to her nest at the top of the tree next to my office under the shed. I contemplated going to the front porch to see what I could pilfer, but the thunder and rain kept me inside. I lit a small fire, turned off my desk lamp, and curled up on the braided rug in front of the fireplace to get a good night's sleep.

And tried not to dream of Lenore.

Made in the USA
Columbia, SC
19 December 2024